POLO'S MOTHER

Books by Phyllis Reynolds Naylor

Witch's Sister
Witch Water
The Witch Herself
Walking Through the Dark
How I Came to Be a Writer
How Lazy Can You Get?
Eddie, Incorporated
All Because I'm Older
Shadows on the Wall
Faces in the Water
Footprints at the Window
The Boy with the Helium Head
A String of Chances
The Solomon System
Bernie Magruder and the Case of the Big Stink
Night Cry
Old Sadie and the Christmas Bear
The Dark of the Tunnel
The Agony of Alice
The Keeper
Bernie Magruder and the Disappearing Bodies
The Year of the Gopher
Beetles, Lightly Toasted
Maudie in the Middle
One of the Third Grade Thonkers
Alice in Rapture, Sort Of
Keeping a Christmas Secret
Bernie Magruder and the Haunted Hotel
Send No Blessings
Reluctantly Alice
King of the Playground
Shiloh
All but Alice
Josie's Troubles
The Grand Escape

POLO'S MOTHER

Phyllis Reynolds Naylor

illustrated by
Alan Daniel

Atheneum Books for Young Readers
NEW YORK   LONDON   TORONTO   SYDNEY

Atheneum Books for Young Readers
An imprint of Simon & Schuster Children's Publishing Division
1230 Avenue of the Americas
New York, New York 10020

The text for this book is set in Goudy.
Manufactured in the United States of America
First Edition
2 4 6 8 10 9 7 5 3 1
Library of Congress Cataloging-in-Publication Data
Naylor, Phyllis Reynolds.
Polo's mother / by Phyllis Reynolds Naylor.—1st ed.
p.   cm.
Summary: Polo finds his mother and tries to impress her with his courage as he and the other members of the Club of Mysteries set out on new adventures.
ISBN 0-689-86555-4
[1. Cats—Fiction. 2. Mothers—Fiction. 3. Adventure and adventurers—Fiction.] I. Title.
PZ7.N24Po 2005
[Fic]—dc22   2003013648

To Garrett Riley Naylor
with apologies to Guinness and Fiona

Contents

POLO'S
MOTHER

1
OUT OF THE NIGHT

When the trees turned feathery green and brooks began to babble, Polo missed his mother. He had been missing her ever since he was a kitten, of course, but spring was especially sad because he had been born in the spring, and all the scents and sounds of the season reminded him of her.

"Can't you stop wriggling about for even a second?" asked Marco from his side of the velveteen basket. "You twist and turn, you snort and sniffle and make all those wretched noises in your sleep. What's the matter?"

"I miss our mother," said Polo. "I'd just like to see her again, that's all."

"She probably wouldn't recognize you," said Marco.

"I know," said Polo.

"Then why do you want to find her?"

"I just want to be near that soft-warm, dark-dank,

1

furry-purry, milk-smelling something again," Polo said.

"Good luck," Marco told him. "There must be five thousand cats in this city."

Polo climbed out of the velveteen box and paced back and forth in front of the dining room windows. The kittens, Jumper and Spinner, were sprawled at either end of the sofa in the next room, and Marco and Polo could hear the soft footsteps of Mrs. Neal as she came downstairs to start the morning coffee.

"My goodness, Polo, do you want to go out so soon?" she asked. "Don't you even want your breakfast first?"

She came through the kitchen in her robe and slippers and unlocked the back door. Marco roused himself also and climbed from the basket. If Polo was going out into the early spring morning to have an adventure, then Marco had to go along. He couldn't bear the thought that his brother, who was usually the more timid of the two, might do something adventurous without him.

"You want to go too?" asked Mrs. Neal. "I don't know . . . Every time I let you cats out, you seem to disappear for a week or so. What you do and where you go is a mystery to me."

She opened the door and the cats went out—first Polo, one paw hesitantly in front of the other, and then Marco, who stopped on the threshold to stretch. His hind legs went back, his front legs went forward, and as his belly sank lower and lower toward the floor, his rump went higher and higher. Finally Mrs. Neal put out one foot, gave him a nudge, and closed the door behind him.

• • •

"Now what?" asked Marco as they walked down the path to the back fence. "It's a big, wide world out here, Polo, and we don't even know where we were born. Under somebody's porch, I imagine."

"Maybe we'll find one of our brothers or sisters and they'll know where Mother is," said Polo.

"You don't understand," Marco said as the tabbies leaped up on the gate and over into the alley. "The world is big. The world is huge. Mother could have wandered across town and been adopted by a family there. She could have been living with someone who packed up and moved to Oklahoma! She—"

"Stop!" cried Polo. "She's still around; I'm sure of it!" If anything had happened to their wonderful soft-warm, dark-dank, furry-purry, milk-smelling something, he didn't want to know it.

"Well, because of you, we left the house without breakfast, so we're not having any adventures till I've got something in my stomach," Marco told him. With that he set off down the alley in the direction of the Fishmonger Restaurant, where all the neighborhood cats gathered when they wanted a treat. All they had to do was to nose up the lids of the garbage cans and crawl down inside.

There were no other cats prowling around the garbage cans at this hour, however, as the most fragrant, fishy leftovers did not get thrown out till later in the day. But the tabbies were hungry, and one of the lids was ajar. So Polo, being the more nimble of the two, leaped up on the rim of

3

the first can, nudged the lid over a few more inches, and peered down inside.

"What's on the menu?" asked his pudgier brother from the ground below.

"A bit of buttermilk pancake with maple syrup . . ." said Polo.

"Continue," said Marco.

"Biscuits and gravy . . ."

"Keep going."

"Half a cheese omelet with pork sausage and a piece of bacon with home fries," Polo finished.

"I'll take some of that sausage," said Marco. "If you can mop up a little gravy with it, so much the better."

Polo disappeared down inside the garbage can and came up with a sausage in his mouth and gravy on his whiskers.

"It'll do," said Marco, as Polo dropped the morsel at his brother's feet and went back a second time to fetch his own breakfast.

They ate in silence for a while, snapping at the meat until they had bitten off a hunk. Then they chewed each bite with relish and sat licking their paws and rubbing the fur around their mouths. The sky was growing lighter, the air warmer, the birds became noisier still, and at last the sun peeped over the roofs of the houses across the alley.

"*Now* can we look for Mother?" Polo asked.

"Yes, but now my stomach's full and all I want to do is sleep," Marco told him. "We'll take a little nap first. What got you started on this, anyway?"

"I can smell her scent," said Polo. "The milk—"

"It was the pancake," said Marco.

"No," said Polo. "I can smell the damp—"

"It's probably going to rain," said his brother.

"No," said Polo. "The scent of warm skin—"

"It's the sun coming out on the shingles. Let's head back down the alley to Murphy's garage and see if anyone there has seen her," Marco suggested. "Maybe one of the other cats knows our mother."

So they trotted back down the alley, tails in the air, until they came to Mr. Murphy's garage. In they went and up the narrow, dusty stairs to the floor above.

"You're late!" boomed a voice from out of the shadows. And there, in an old rocking chair, sat a yellow cat, one paw dangling over the side. He was a big cat, a banged-up cat, who had obviously been through a few fights in his life. He looked at the two tabby brothers with his large, yellow eyes and repeated, "You're late! The moon was full last night, so where were you?"

Ever since Marco and Polo had been admitted to the Club of Mysteries, Texas Jake had tried to ridicule Marco, because he was smart, and Polo, because he wasn't.

"Oh, Texas, do be kind!" said the beautiful calico cat named Carlotta, who was the friend of all but the true love of none. "I'm glad to see you, Marco. You too, Polo. We've *all* missed you, haven't we?" She looked around at Boots, the white cat with the brown paws, and Elvis, the sleek black cat with the green eyes. Boots just turned his head and looked the other way, while Elvis began to groom himself, licking between his claws with his long, pink tongue.

5

The truth was that none of the male cats was particularly eager to share the lovely Carlotta with anyone else, but because Marco and Polo had passed the test for membership, they were members of the club, like it or not.

When Carlotta sidled up to Marco, however, and rubbed noses, then walked over to lick Polo on the head, Texas Jake rose up to his full height on the rocker, his stiff leg notwithstanding, and growled.

"Just the same, Carlotta, we are a club, and a club must have rules!" he hissed. "This club is to meet on the first night of a full moon, and last night the tabbies were not here. What is required of cats who are not here?"

Boots and Elvis raised their heads and joined Texas in answer: "Solve another mystery."

"It's all my fault!" Polo said quickly. "My mind was on other things."

Texas Jake settled down in his chair and seemed to be enjoying himself now. "Ah! So his mind was on other things! Your mind is so small, Polo, what would such a mind be on? An acorn? A pea? A grain of sand?"

"Hush, Texas," said Carlotta. "What's the matter, Polo? What's troubling you?"

Polo looked around at the group of cats, who were all staring at him now. "I want to find my mother," he said. When the cats continued to stare, he added, "I know she must be around here *some*where."

"What's her name?" asked Boots.

"I don't know," said Polo.

"What does she look like?" asked Elvis.

"I don't know," said Polo.

"How many kittens were in your litter?" asked Carlotta.

"I don't know that, either," said Polo miserably.

Texas Jake—Lord of the Loft, King of the Alley, Commander in Chief, and Cat Supreme—scoffed. "Then how do you ever expect to find her, this mother of yours?" he jeered. "Perhaps your brother—the cat who can reeeeeead—should put an ad in the paper!"

But Carlotta snuggled up against Polo there on the floor of the loft. "We'll help you find her," she said. "Because if my kittens ever look for me, I hope someone will help them, too. Do you remember anything about your mother, Polo? What was she like?"

"She was soft and warm and dark and dank; she was furry and purry and smelled of milk," Polo told her.

"Hmmmm," said Carlotta, but her eyes were beginning to close as a beam of sunlight came through the open window at one end of the garage, falling on her head and paws. She slept. The other cats, Texas included, hopped down to share the sunbeam, stretching out on their backs or bellies, and purred with pleasure. As the sunlight moved across the floor, the cats moved with it. Finally, when it disappeared, they roused themselves and went to the Fishmonger for dinner.

There was time only for a short snack, however— a bit of flounder and a shrimp or two—for Marco had been right: Despite the sun during the day, rain was in the air. A chilly wind blew in from the west, and cold spring rain fell in a steady shower from the sky. The cats in the Club of Mysteries scampered back to the loft and prepared to bed down for the night.

"There still need to be rules," Texas Jake said when he had everyone's attention. "Marco and Polo will have to solve another mystery if they are to remain members in good standing."

Marco had never liked the bossy cat, and he liked him even less now. But he did not want the other cats to think he could not solve another of life's mysteries, so he said, "Okay, bring it on, Texas. What mystery do you have in mind?"

"I'll think about it," the big yellow cat replied, meaning he would give them the most difficult mystery possible.

The rain fell, *rat-a-tat, rat-a-tat,* on the roof. It dropped, *pit-a-pat, pit-a-pat,* from the eaves onto the soft ground below. The cats—all but Texas, who claimed the rocker as his throne—looked about the loft for a place to settle down and began to groom themselves.

As the other club members dropped off to sleep, Marco stayed awake for some time. Now that Polo had brought it up, he, too, wondered about their mother. There were so many things—awful things—that could happen to a cat. She could have been in a fight with mangy old Steak Knife and his Over-the-Hill Gang at the dump. She could have been mauled by the huge neighborhood mastiff, Bertram the Bad; she could have been attacked by the river rats or taken to the pound.

The safest place in the world for a cat was probably

back in the home of Mr. and Mrs. Neal, where Marco and Polo belonged, where the kittens Jumper and Spinner lived. Even up here in the loft, away from cars and trucks and dogs and rats, bad things could happen.

Cats would be cats, however, and the brothers liked to roam, yet deep down inside, where not even Polo could see, Marco had to admit that even he missed the soft-warm, dark-dank, furry-purry, milk-smelling something they called Mother. And he wondered whether, if they found her, they could take her home to live with them at the Neals' or keep her here in the loft and protect her always.

But finally Marco's eyes began to close and he, too, fell asleep.

The rain went on falling, *rat-a-tat*, on the roof. The water continued to drip, *pit-a-pat*, onto the ground. A chill night breeze blew in the open window of the loft, ruffling the fur on the backs of the sleeping felines so that they curled their heads under their paws and drew themselves up into tight little balls.

Far down the alley, a large, wet, scraggly, scratchety silhouette of a cat came moping and loping along in the shadows, slinking along through the rain, creeping behind barrels and boxes and trash cans and bags of old winter leaves.

It paused for a moment, looking behind it toward the darkness of the dump, then looking ahead toward the Fishmonger. It sniffed the air and glanced up toward the open window of the garage. Finally, its fur dark and wet, its breath fishy and stale, its claws jagged and dirty, its paws callused and bruised, it left the mysteries of the alley and ducked into the doorway of Murphy's garage. Then, sniffing still, it moved noiselessly up the stairs to the loft.

2

GERALDINE

Polo opened one eye and sniffed.

The dump.

He opened the other eye and sniffed again.

The river.

Outside the loft, the birds called to each other, declaring this tree or that private property, announcing that this bush or that shrub was taken. The sun was not yet up, but the sky was beginning to lighten, and Polo could make out the shapes of the other cats who were sprawled here and there—Texas Jake on the rocker, Elvis on the army cot, Boots on an old suitcase, Marco asleep on a pile of newspapers, Carlotta beside him.

But now Marco, too, raised his head and sniffed. And then, as though the scent were traveling around the loft, touching each cat in turn on the nose, one after another the cats rose and looked around.

"I smell the dump," said Texas, his hair beginning to rise, thinking of the cat named Steak Knife.

"I smell the river," said Boots, his tail beginning to thicken, thinking of rats.

"I smell the Fishmonger, too, and a bit of the alley," said Carlotta.

"The woods!" said Elvis. "I smell wet leaves and grass and pinecones and bark."

"And fleas," said Marco, hoisting a hind leg and scratching himself behind one ear. "Don't forget fleas."

They turned their heads this way and that, their noses twitching like little black beetles, to see whether a stranger was present, but everything looked the same as before—the lamp with the torn shade, the trunk with the rusted latch, the birdcage, the old fur coat, the work shoes, the flower pots.

"What is it, Texas?" Boots asked, looking toward the big yellow cat in the rocker. "Do you think Steak Knife came by in the night and discovered where the Club of Mysteries meets?"

"If he has, he'll be back, I'll wager, his flea-bitten band of scoundrels with him," said Texas Jake.

"Maybe the river rats paid us a visit while we were sleeping," said Elvis. "Everybody check your paws; make sure they haven't nibbled one or made off with your tail."

"If it's tails someone's after, that would be Steak Knife," said Polo, remembering how one of Carlotta's kittens had almost lost its tail to Steak Knife's collection there at the dump.

All at once there was a slight rustling noise in one corner of the loft, and suddenly, up out of the rag box rose a ghastly apparition of old shirts and socks and a sweater or two. Then, as the garments slid off, one by one, there in the rag box sat a large gray cat with green eyes and white whiskers about the mouth. The fur on its back was beginning to thin, and the tufts of hair on its head stuck up in unruly patches here and there. The big gray cat opened its mouth, showed its yellow teeth, and meowed a loud "*Quiet!*"

The other cats jumped in astonishment.

"Steak Knife?" said Boots in fright.

Only Polo stepped forward. "Mo-ther!" he cried.

While the others stared, the large she-cat climbed out of the rag box where Carlotta had once brought her kittens. She lumbered across the floor to where Polo stood trembling and gave his rump a sniff.

"Must be one of mine," she meowed, and then she yawned. "All this yammering and mewing and yowling and fussing! Can't an old mother cat get herself a good night's sleep in a dry place without a bunch of young upstarts filling the air with nonsense?"

At that, Texas Jake rose on his rocker, as tall as his toes would allow him, his fur standing on end, which made him seem even larger and taller than he was.

"Do you know where you are, madam, and do you know who I am?" he thundered.

"I seem to be in a garage of some sort with a pip-squeak here who claims to be my son, and I don't know *you* from a hole in the ground," the gray cat answered.

The other cats were shocked that this stranger would speak to their leader in such a way, but no more surprised than Texas Jake himself.

13

"I," he said, his huge head erect, his eyes wide with indignation, "am Texas Jake, Lord of the Loft, King of the Alley, Commander in Chief, the Cat Supreme."

"I don't care if you're King Tut," said the gray cat. "I'm Geraldine, mother of twenty-nine kittens, give or take a few, so I guess I know something about life that an old warrior like you can't appreciate."

The cats in the Club of Mysteries stared in disbelief. Texas Jake leaped to the floor despite the injuries he had suffered over the years and began circling Polo's mother, a low growl coming from his throat. Now the cats were truly unnerved, for Geraldine, instead of lying down on her belly and acting sorry, began to growl in return, the fur rising on the back of *her* scruffy neck, and *she* began circling too.

"Stop!" yelled Marco.

Texas Jake and Geraldine stopped in their tracks.

"Don't tell me this is another one of my brood," said Geraldine. "They always *were* a noisy bunch, all six batches of them."

Marco and Polo approached the large gray cat who had turned now to look at them. Polo closed his eyes when he got closer and drank in her smell—her soft-warm, dark-dank, furry-purry, milk-smelling scent, all mixed up with a dump-river-fish-woods-leaves-bark smell.

"Mother!" Polo said again, burying his face in her furry side to breathe in that wonderful scent, and Geraldine gave him a dutiful lick on the ear.

"I suppose you want one too," she said to Marco.

He did, actually, though he was embarrassed to accept

her affection in front of the other members of the Club of Mysteries. But he bent his head to receive her lick and then stood back as Geraldine stretched her body out long and gave an enormous yawn.

"Well," she said, looking about her. "Every few years I try to make the rounds of all the places I've ever lived— look up my kittens, if I can find them, and see how they're doing. You two have found yourselves a tidy place to stay. It's dry, it's warm, and there's the Fishmonger down the alley. I trust you can occasionally find a mouse or two up here for a snack, because I could do with a little mousey morsel about now."

"Madam," said Texas Jake, asserting himself again. "Mother or no mother, you should be informed that this is more than a 'tidy place.' We are the Club of Mysteries, and no one can lodge here who is not a member in good standing."

"Hogwash," said Geraldine.

"Don't worry, Mother. If you want to be a member, we'll help get you in," said Polo.

"What do you mean, 'in'? I *am* in," said Geraldine. "I'm as 'in' as a cat can be. Just let King Tut here try to push me out! Just let him try! I've scratched out more eyes than he has hairs on his body, I can tell you!"

This time Texas Jake's ears flattened against his head, and he turned to Marco. "Perhaps Marco—your son who can reeeeeead—might enlighten you," he said with a sneer.

The gray cat with the green eyes stared at Marco. "Well, *that's* a wonder!" she said. "He certainly never learned that from me. How did that happen?"

Marco was truly embarrassed now. He did not want

16

the other cats to know exactly how he had taught himself to read, but Geraldine's eyes were on him.

"The litter box," he said softly.

At that, all the cats in the Club of Mysteries, all but Polo, meowed in merriment.

"The *litter* box?" Geraldine repeated.

Marco stared down at his paws. "The newspaper at the bottom of the box," he said. "I simply paid attention, that's all."

"And Polo?" the mother cat asked, turning to her other son.

"I just did my business and climbed out," Polo admitted, and once again the other cats grinned and meowed softly among themselves.

All but Carlotta. She went over to the tabby brothers and said, "It's all right. One cat who can read is enough, and we're glad to have you both in the Club of Mysteries." And then, turning to Texas Jake, she said, "I think there should be a clause in our rules that all mothers are to be admitted without having to solve any mystery at all."

This, however, made Geraldine rise indignantly. "Do you think I can't keep up with the rest of you?" she said, her fur ruffled. "Whatever it is you have to do to be a member of this silly crew, do you think this old she-cat is too old to learn new tricks? Bring it on, Texas-what's-your-name! I'm ready! What do I have to do?"

Texas Jake hunkered back down on the rocker, and his yellow eyes narrowed to small slits. "Very well, Geraldine. Solve this one: What is dust?"

"Dust?" cried the gray cat, sitting down hard on her

17

haunches. "Why, everyone knows that dust is made up of cat hair, dog hair, and little star babies falling out of the sky."

She spoke with such assurance that Texas Jake was taken aback. Who could doubt a cat who seemed such an authority on dust?

"That was only a test," he said. "Try this one: If two-leggeds wear things over their eyes to help them see better, and things inside their ears to help them hear better, why don't they wear things over their noses to help them smell better?"

Polo, who had snuggled as close to his mother as he dared without getting a swat from her paw, thought that a most interesting question. Why, indeed? Did humans not want to smell as well as four-leggeds, who could detect Kentucky Fried Chicken three blocks away?

But Geraldine seemed to know the answer to that one also. "Pshaw!" she said. "Can't you do better than that, Texas? There's nothing to *hang* it on, that's why! The ears hold their glasses in place, and their hearing aids fit down inside their ears, but what could they do for the nose? If you stuck something inside it, the something would fall right out. Two-leggeds can only *wish* they could smell as well as we can, Texas Jake. Don't bore me with these silly questions."

She stretched out on the floor, taking up the whole patch of sunshine for herself, and began to lick her paws.

Texas Jake was losing ground, and he had to do something. "All right, Geraldine. Here is your mystery to solve," he said. "When two-leggeds close the door of a refrigerator, does the light stay on or not? And you cannot make a guess. For this one you have to find out for yourself."

18

Polo's heart sank. It did not take a cat as smart as Marco to know that the only way to prove *that* was to be *inside* a refrigerator when someone closed the door. Texas Jake had a way of giving dangerous, almost unsolvable mysteries to the cats he hoped never to see again, and Geraldine was certainly one of them.

The old gray cat's eyes began to close, and her paws stretched out in front of her, the claws extending and retracting. "In due time," she purred. "In due time."

And Polo, lying down beside her, snuggled a little closer to that soft-warm, dark-dank, furry-purry, milk-smelling creature he remembered as Mother. She wasn't exactly the mother he'd expected, the mother he'd hoped she would be, but Geraldine would do.

3
MOTHER O' MINE

When the cats set out for the Fishmonger that evening, Polo could not help himself; he wanted to introduce Geraldine to everyone he met. He *did* have a mother, and she *did* remember him, sort of, and she *had* licked his ear.

The first creature they met was a large black crow, who kept one beady eye on the goings-on in the alley and the other eye on the lookout for any tasty morsel, dead or dying, that he might like to sample.

"Crow!" called Polo when he saw him. "Come here and meet my mother!"

"*Your* mother?" said Marco sharply.

"*Our* mother," Polo said. "Marco's and mine."

The crow hopped down from the fence post on which he had perched. He studied Geraldine with one eye, then, turning his head, the other.

"You look as though you've seen a lot of life," the crow said.

"I've been around," said Geraldine.

"A few battles now and then?"

"I've had my share."

"You don't have any kittens who are doing poorly, do you?" the crow asked. "Any who might . . . uh . . . to put it delicately . . . be departing this life and would make a tasty appetizer for the likes of me?"

Polo was horrified that the crow would even suggest such a thing. Geraldine, however, didn't bat an eye.

"Watch your tongue," she said, glancing toward Carlotta. "There's a young mother present. My job is to bring kittens into this world, and what happens to them after that, I don't usually know."

"Well, *my* job is animal removal," said the crow. "If it weren't for the crows of this world, you would be belly-deep in roadkill. But you," he said, studying Geraldine more closely, "you yourself have seen better days, I would guess. Hair beginning to thin? Feeling a bit wobbly in the legs?"

"I beg your pardon?" said Geraldine coldly. "I'll wager I'm as strong as you are."

"A pity," said the crow.

"Could we talk about something else?" Polo pleaded, and the bird immediately bowed and said his good-bye.

"Most pleased, indeed, to make your acquaintance," he said to Geraldine.

And then, with a great flapping of wings, the crow rose from the cement of the alley, up and up, soaring over the roofs of the houses beyond. But Polo noticed that

21

after circling a time or two, the crow came back. He lit on a telephone pole not far away and kept one beady eye on Geraldine.

"He's awful," Polo murmured to his brother.

"He's a crow," Marco answered.

The cats were not halfway down the alley when suddenly their mother pounced. She moved so fast that the tabbies did not even see it coming and were startled to find a limp gray mouse dangling from her jaws.

"Timothy!" cried Polo. "Don't eat him, Mother. He's my friend!"

"Your *what?*" Geraldine said, whereupon the small gray mouse dropped from her mouth and raced to the safety of a fallen garbage can lid.

"Our friend," Texas Jake said, answering for him. "We've been tempted once or twice to eat him, but the little tyke has helped us out a time or two, so he's not to be touched. He is not to be thought of as an appetizer, an entrée, a salad, or a dessert. Not even an after-dinner mint. As long as Timothy lives, he shall have the protection of the Club of Mysteries."

Geraldine made a face and gagged a little. "Just as well," she said. "His feet were dirty. Long tails I can abide, but one thing I can't stand is gritty feet."

"Timothy, this is our mother, Marco's and mine," Polo said in a belated introduction.

"And may we always be ten paw-lengths apart," said the little mouse from beneath the garbage can lid.

It was a fine night for dinner out. The moon was full, rising white and round over the telephone poles, and, as usual, the most delicious aromas came from the restaurant.

"'Friday Night Flounder Feast,'" Marco read from the banner over the door. "'All You Can Eat.'"

Geraldine stared. "That's what it says? The black marks on white paper say all that?"

"Ah, yes, Geraldine, you have birthed a cat who can reeeeeead," said Texas Jake. "And he has gotten no further in life than the rest of us."

"I know what's going on in the world," Marco protested.

"And what does that bring you but worry?" asked Elvis.

"I know where there is wet paint and when not to walk on the grass and where there is a dog to beware of," said Marco.

"Why, we can tell you the very same things with a mere sniff of our noses, a twitch of our ears, and our two green eyes," said Elvis.

"Never mind," Geraldine said to Marco. "I have always had a fancy to read a story before I go to sleep. Perhaps you can find a story to read to me sometime, Marco."

"A pleasure," Marco answered.

Polo was instantly jealous. He could not bear to think that his mother might prefer Marco to him and immediately resolved that he would do something—*some*thing—to make her proud of him, too.

But meanwhile there were other friends who needed introducing, and he was happy to see the Cat Quartet, of which Elvis was a member. The Persian, the Siamese, and the Abyssinian immediately hissed, their fur rising on their backs, when an old gray cat walked toward them from across the parking lot of the Fishmonger. But Polo called out, "Boys, I'd like you to meet my mother. Marco's mother as well. She's staying with us at the Club of Mysteries, and her name is Geraldine."

Slowly the cats settled down and came over to give Geraldine a polite sniff.

"And in honor of the occasion, tonight is Friday Night Flounder Feast," said Marco.

That cheered the group considerably, for an "all-you-can-eat" banquet meant that the two-leggeds always took more than they should and left a lot on their plates. Every little bit left over found its way into the garbage cans behind the Fishmonger, and every cat found his way into the dark, fish-smelling cans to eat until his tummy could hold no more.

"What would you like, Mother? I'll get it for you," Polo said. "Flounder, crab, perch, or salmon? Just name it."

"Thank you, Polo, but I prefer to help myself," Geraldine said, whereupon she lowered her body into a crouch, then sprang to the rim of the nearest can, pushed over the lid with her nose, and disappeared inside.

An all-you-can-eat night brought out the best in the cats, and—the night air being delightful too—all the cats large and small, young and old, fat and skinny seemed to want to linger on the warm concrete of the parking lot. They soon gathered near the wall at the back to lick their paws and chat.

"So this is your mother!" purred the Persian, surveying Geraldine. "I think this calls for a celebration, Polo. *I* think it calls for a song."

"A song! A song!" the other cats meowed, and Polo was

24

delighted that his mother should be honored in this way.

There was nothing Elvis liked better than to perform in front of an audience, the bigger the better. The sleek black cat with the green eyes rose up on his toes and said, "For you, Geraldine, the Cat Quartet will compose something special. Let us have a few minutes to prepare, if you please."

At that, the Cat Quartet disappeared over the wall, and all that could be seen of Elvis, the Siamese, the Persian, and the Abyssinian were their tails. When they returned, they took their places up on the wall, waiting until a couple of two-leggeds in a blue car had gotten out and gone inside the Fishmonger.

Then Elvis stepped forward. "For Polo's mother," he said, "the Cat Quartet will sing 'Mother o' Mine.'" The four cats sat side by side on the wall, their heads together, and when the Abyssinian gave the pitch, they all began to meow at once:

> "Oh, we love the dear silver that shines in your fur,
> The brow that's all wrinkled, the warmth of your purr,
> We love the quick gleam in your green eyes so kind,
> Oh, God bless you and keep you, Mother o' Mine."

All the cats howled their appreciation—all, that is, but Geraldine. "Excuse me, gents, but what's this about silver in my fur? A wrinkled brow? A *gleam*, did you say? I'll admit I'm no spring chicken, but I'm a long way from a crow's dinner, I can tell you. How about something a bit snappier, a bit more lively, something with pizzazz, for dog's sake?"

The Cat Quartet was surprised at this, for they were not used to being unappreciated and weren't at all sure about this cat named Geraldine. Nonetheless, once again all you could see of their tails were the tips as they disappeared over the top of the wall. And once again the other cats waited, licking their paws, while the Cat Quartet composed a new song.

This time when the four reappeared, they did not sit down on the wall; they stood. And they didn't just stand; they pranced as they sang:

> "She's a grand old cat,
> She's a high-flying cat,
> And forever in peace may she prowl.
> She's the emblem of
> The cats we love,
> The moms with the lighthearted meow.
> Every heart beats true
> For the mom who can chew
> On a bug or a bee or bat.
> Should old acquaintance be forgot
> Keep your eye on that grand old cat."

"Now that's more like it!" said Geraldine.

But Texas Jake, clearly, was not pleased. If anybody should be referred to as the "grand old cat," the "high-flying cat," it was he. He hadn't become Lord of the Loft, King of the Alley, Commander in Chief, and Cat Supreme by doing nothing. What about all of *his* brave deeds—the times he had saved the Club of Mysteries from certain disaster? He

27

wasn't about to be cast aside for a scruffy old she-cat who thought she could just flounce in without so much as an "if you please."

"Oh, Geraldine," said Carlotta, walking over and rubbing up against the old cat's side, "we're so glad to have you in our club. It will be wonderful having another female around."

Texas Jake rose up high on his toes, his back arched. "She's not a member yet," he hissed, his cold yellow eyes on Geraldine. Her green eyes stared back, and Polo saw there was an icy gleam in them. Definitely a gleam.

4
A BOLD PLAN

Texas Jake was all business when the cats got back to Murphy's garage. As moonlight streamed through the open window at one end of the loft, he took his place on the rocker, one paw hanging over the edge, and surveyed the cats gathered on the floor below him with his big yellow eyes.

"Geraldine," he said, addressing the gray cat, who seemed more intent on cleaning between her toes than on paying attention to him, "you may have taught your twenty-nine kittens many things, but one thing you did *not* teach them was promptness."

"Ha!" said Geraldine. "Just *you* try raising twenty-nine kittens, buster, and see how well *you* do."

Texas Jake ignored her. "Promptness is a virtue, Geraldine, and one that cannot be overlooked."

"If that's the only thing I overlooked, I was a very good

29

mother indeed," Geraldine responded, fixing her great green eyes on him.

"Nevertheless," said Texas Jake, "rules are rules, and Marco and Polo knew that they were to be here when the moon was full. They were not here, however—all the rest of us had gathered—and so, in order to remain members in good standing of the Club of Mysteries, each of them must solve another mystery."

"Whatever," said Geraldine, and concentrated on removing a small piece of salmon stuck between her claws.

"Just tell us what mysteries need solving, Texas Jake, and get it over with," said Marco impatiently.

"All right, here it is," said Texas. "You, Marco, oh cat who can reeeeeead, must tell us what it is, exactly, under the hood of a car that makes it purr. And you, Polo, must tell us what is at the very tip-top of a church steeple. Something very important must be up there for the two-leggeds to build it so high."

All the cats knew at once how Texas Jake felt about the striped tabbies and their mother. Boots and Elvis and Texas himself had only had to lie on their backs in the sun and ponder a mystery, while the tabbies had to go out on dangerous missions to find the answers to theirs—Geraldine to the inside of a refrigerator, Marco under the hood of a car, and Polo to the top of a church steeple.

"Oh, Texas," cried Carlotta, who had been admitted to membership without solving any mystery at all, simply because the beautiful calico she-cat was—well, Carlotta, and that was enough. "Those are dangerous missions, and we might never see our tabbies again!"

Texas Jake could not suppress a smile. "Is that a fact?" he said. "Well, Polo is nimble, Geraldine is wise—*old* enough to be wise, anyway—and Marco can reeeeeeead! They ought to be able to tell us the answers to these mysteries and still have one of their nine lives left, I would imagine."

With that, he gave an enormous yawn, rolled over on his side, stretched out his paws, and went to sleep.

The other cats found places in the loft to settle down for the night—an old stack of newspapers, the army cot, an ancient fur coat, a pile of old shoes. Geraldine climbed into the rag box where she had slept her first night in the garage, and, without asking, Polo crawled in beside her. She had not exactly invited him, but she let him snuggle down next to her just the same.

"Do you think you can do it, Mother?" he asked in a small voice. "Do you think you can get inside a refrigerator and find out whether the light stays on? I will do everything I can to help you. I'll even crawl in *for* you, if you'll let me."

"I can get *in*. The question is, can I get *out*?" Geraldine said. "No, Polo, this is my problem to solve, and I'm not about to let that big Texas windbag have the last word. I didn't raise twenty-nine kittens for nothing. I think I've learned a *little* something."

Was there anything as wonderful as a mother? Polo thought as he buried his nose even deeper into her fur. How he had missed her all this time! What a wonderful stroke of luck that here she was, lying beside him in the rag box. Heaven could be no better than this.

31

And Marco, though he'd never spoken much about their mother, must have been feeling the same, because sometime that evening, Polo felt a nudge as his brother climbed in beside him and snuggled down too against their mother. And for the rest of the night, Polo dreamed of being a kitten again, of his mother's rough, red tongue on the top of his head, and of the low purr coming from deep inside her warm body.

When they woke the next morning, Geraldine was gone. Texas Jake looked about the loft and sneered.

"Do you see what stuff you tabbies are made of?" he scoffed. "She's taken off, mates. Absconded. Skidooed. Give her a job and what does she do? Disappears. Knows she can't do it, so off she goes."

Polo opened his eyes and sat up. Gone? So soon? His mother was gone? He could not bear it. All these months he had been thinking about her, and she was gone, like a weed in the wind.

"Well, lads?" Texas said, turning his gaze to Marco and Polo. "I suppose you're next, eh? Marco will never be able to tell us what makes a car purr, and Polo will never find out what is at the top of a church steeple. If you want to leave now, lads, go."

But before either of the tabbies could answer, there was a soft pawstep on the stairs, and into the loft stepped the old gray cat.

"All right, Texas Jake," she said. "I have found a house that keeps a refrigerator on the back porch. If you'd care to move your big self off that rocker and follow me for a

32

few blocks, I'll find a way to get inside it, and then I can tell you whether the light stays on or goes off when the door is closed, seeing as how this is so important to you."

Polo was so glad to see his mother that he scampered across the floor to snuggle against her, but she was all business and swatted him away with her paw.

Actually, Texas Jake had been looking forward to breakfast at the Fishmonger—a little sushi, perhaps, or a sardine or two. But here was this old gray cat insisting he come watch her solve her mystery, so he gave his paws a quick once-over and, with the other cats walking behind, followed Geraldine down the dusty stairs of the loft and out the door of Murphy's garage.

Geraldine seemed to know the alley as well as any cat there. She looked both ways before crossing the street; she circled the potholes on the other side, flattened herself against a garage when a delivery truck rumbled by, and remembered which yards had dogs that would bark at her as she passed.

At last they came to a small yard where a tiny brown-and-yellow house sat close to the alley. There was a low back porch, and on the porch sat two folding chairs, an old, torn couch, and a refrigerator with a cord leading up to a light socket.

The refrigerator was making a humming sound, so it must be in working order, the cats decided. The house was so small that the only good place for the refrigerator was the back porch.

"Well, Geraldine, what do you do next?" Texas Jake asked.

"Here's the plan," she told them. "We wait until the lady of the house comes out to get something. As soon as she opens the door, Polo, you must leap up on her head and stay there long enough to distract her so that I can dart onto the bottom shelf and hide behind the lettuce or whatever the two-leggeds keep in there."

Polo was delighted to have been asked to help, but Marco said, "Mother, once she closes the door again, how will you get out?"

"When the lady of the house comes out again, I'll simply scramble out with the answer to the mystery. It's breakfast time for the two-leggeds, and you know how often they open and close their refrigerators at breakfast."

That was true. All the cats in the Club of Mysteries, with the exception of Geraldine, perhaps, had homes with masters or mistresses, and they all knew about the habits of two-leggeds.

"An excellent plan, Geraldine," said Texas Jake. "Very good indeed." The big yellow cat led the others over to the row of shrubs at one side of the yard and hid themselves, leaving only Polo and his mother crouched beside the porch steps.

The sky was just beginning to lighten, and most of the houses on the alley were still dark. Now and then a light came on in a window, and in a little while the wonderful aroma of sizzling bacon came wafting by on the breeze.

At long last, just as the first rays of sun showed through the branches of a maple tree, a light came on in the kitchen of the small brown-and-yellow house, and then the back door opened.

Out stepped—not the lady of the house—but a boy of about ten. He was wearing racing car pajamas and flip-flops on his feet. Sleepily, he rubbed his eyes with one hand and reached for the handle of the refrigerator with the other. He paused a moment for a gigantic yawn, then opened the door.

Polo sprang. He landed on top of the boy's head, clinging tightly to the thick brown hair so he wouldn't fall off.

The boy in the racing car pajamas howled as though he were being carried off by a giant falcon. His eyes were as large as two fried eggs, and he stood bellowing with his arms straight out at his sides, too frightened to reach up and see what was roosting on his head.

In those few seconds Geraldine leaped inside the refrigerator and crept behind a package of hamburger buns and a jar of pickles. Once she was safely inside, Polo jumped to the ground and dashed behind the bushes where the other cats were waiting, while the boy on the porch continued to howl.

The back door of the house opened again, and a woman asked, "Bobby, what are you *doing*?"

"A monster had me by the hair!" the boy cried, bellowing still.

"You must be half asleep," his mother said, coming out onto the porch and shutting the door to the refrigerator. "I told you we'll be having breakfast on the road. There's no time for juice. Put on your clothes and get in the car. We have a long drive ahead of us."

And as the members of the Club of Mysteries watched in horror, the two went back inside, then came out again with a suitcase and locked the door behind them. They climbed into the car at the back of the garden, rolled down the windows, and away they went.

5
One Cold Cat

"Mo-ther!" Polo wailed.

Marco, too, was stunned. It had seemed such a bold but reasonable thing to do. The two-leggeds *always* hung around their refrigerator at breakfast time. First the orange juice, then the milk, then the butter, the bacon, the eggs . . .

But if a family left the house with a suitcase, who knew how long they might be gone! Certainly overnight. Maybe a week. A month, even!

"Meow," came a muffled cry from inside the refrigerator.

The cats scampered across the yard and up onto the back porch. Everyone looked concerned except Texas Jake, who, try as he would, could not hide the smile—the smirk—that stretched across his face.

"Well, lads," he said, trying his best to sound sorrowful. "I'm afraid that's that. She was a good cat, a wise cat, a noble cat, and I'm sure we shall all miss her. But every dog has its day, and every cat its fifteen minutes of fame. Except, in the case of your dear mother, fifteen minutes, I'm afraid, may freeze her whiskers."

"We can't just leave her in there, Texas!" Carlotta cried.

"Did *we* put her there, my dear?" asked Texas Jake, his eyes wide with innocence. "Did I even *ask* her to climb inside a refrigerator and put herself in harm's way? No, I did not. I merely gave her a mystery to solve, however she might decide to do it, a mystery we have all wondered about, a question that has been burning inside our brains for lo, these many years. Just *how* she should go about solving the mystery was entirely up to her. Obviously, being a cat of no great intelligence—for what tabby is?—she took it upon herself to climb *inside* a refrigerator, and I'm afraid we all know what can happen to a cat at forty degrees without water for a week or more."

"*Meow!*" came the faraway sound of a furious cat at forty degrees.

Polo was frantic, but already Boots and Elvis were losing interest and had turned their heads toward the Fishmonger, their noses twitching, sniffing the air. The tabby brothers, however, would not dream of leaving their mother.

"Sure, Texas, just walk off and leave her!" Marco said angrily. "How else was she supposed to find out whether the light stays on or goes off?"

"Why, lads, that's where intelligence and creativity come in," said the large cat. "But in the meantime, I think I must feed my brain cells, though I'm sure that you, being cats of great sensitivity, will stay with your mother until the cold, bitter end. Come along, Carlotta. When the door is opened

38

at last, it will not be a sight for pretty little eyes like yours."

So saying, Texas Jake set off down the alley with Boots and Elvis, Carlotta following reluctantly behind.

"*Meow!*" came the cry from inside the refrigerator.

"Mother," meowed Marco. "Can you hear us?"

There was a thud from inside the thick white walls of the refrigerator, like a cat throwing herself against the door, but nothing happened.

Another thud, then another and another, but the door did not open. All Geraldine was doing was exhausting herself, the tabby brothers knew.

"If we were two-leggeds, we could reach that handle and open the door," said Polo.

"If we were two-leggeds with opposable thumbs and fingers, we could pry open the door even if we couldn't reach the handle," said Marco.

"If we had *what?*" asked Polo. Because Marco could read, he knew a great deal more than Polo could ever begin to know, and Polo was in awe of his brother.

"A finger and a thumb opposite each other," Marco explained. "That's how the two-leggeds can do so much. They can pinch things, pound things, pour things, pick things up. Those of us with paws and claws have advantages, to be sure, but we will never be able to grasp things, and that makes all the difference."

Another meow came from deep within the refrigerator, followed by another couple of thumps. But as the minutes passed, Polo could not bear to listen to his mother's cries, and he went out into the alley. He lay down with his head on his paws.

39

"What's the matter?" asked a tiny voice, and Polo opened one eye to see Timothy, the mouse, within inches of his whiskers.

"My mother," Polo said. He explained how she had crawled into the refrigerator to find the answer to a mystery and now was trapped.

"What we need is Crow," said Timothy.

"How can *he* help?" Polo wondered.

"I'm not sure, but with his sharp beak he may be able to do *some*thing," Timothy said.

"Where would we find him?" Polo asked. "We have to work fast, Timothy."

"We don't find Crow. He finds us," said Timothy. "All we have to do is play dead. You watch for cars and dogs and boys on skateboards, and I'll play dead."

With that, Timothy stretched himself out in the middle of the alley, his eyes closed, his little tongue hanging out, and lay as still as a stone.

A minute went by, then two, then three, but at last a shadow fell across the alley as a pair of wings flapped their way down. A moment later the great black crow came gliding out of the sky and landed a few feet away.

The crow stood perfectly still for a moment or two, one yellow eye on Timothy. Then, cocking his head to one side, he took a few steps forward on his sticklike legs, looked at Polo, and said, "Is he dead? How long has he been marinating in the sun?"

"He's not dead," said Polo as Timothy scrambled to his feet, lest the crow decide to taste him anyway.

40

"Well, that's not playing fair!" the crow protested. "Dead is supposed to be dead."

"Oh, please don't hurt him," said Polo. "It was the only way we could think of to bring you here. We desperately need your help."

"And what would that be?" asked Crow, his breast swelling with self-importance.

"It's Geraldine, my mother," Polo told him. "She's trapped in the refrigerator over there on the porch, and the owner has gone off on a trip. Is there anything you can do to get her out?"

"Hmmm," said Crow. "An interesting question. If I leave her there, I'll be assured of dinner in a week or two. But by then she'll be frozen solid, and I never did like my dinners cold. Oh, all right. I'm a crow, not a jackhammer, but I'll see what I can do."

Back they went to the porch, where Marco was keeping vigil by the refrigerator.

"Is she still alive?" asked Crow.

Another meow and an angry thud told them all they needed to know.

Crow walked jerkily around the refrigerator, from one side to the other, pointing each yellow foot out in front of him as he moved, cocking his head and staring at the big, white box with first one eye, then the other.

At last he walked over to where the edge of the door met the body of the refrigerator and thrust his long beak into the crack. He pried and he twisted, he pushed and he pecked, but the door didn't open. Fluttering his wings, he flew a few inches off the floor and tried another place, then another, his wings batting furiously all the while. When he grew tired, he came back down to the floor to rest, then up again he went, beak prying, wings flapping. Finally, finally there was the sound of the rubber seal pulling away from the enamel, and suddenly the door opened just a crack. Immediately Marco wedged his head inside, pushing the door open wider until at last it swung back.

"Hooray!" squeaked Timothy. "Crow, you did it!"

At first they could not see Geraldine, only an overturned bottle of ketchup and a can of peaches. But then one paw emerged from behind the package of hamburger buns, then another, and finally the old gray cat stepped stiffly out of the bottom of the refrigerator, her green eyes large and glassy, her fur cold to the touch.

"She's alive," said Crow, a note of disappointment in his voice.

"Mo-ther!" cried Polo, delighted beyond words.

Geraldine was one cold cat, however. She was not the soft-warm, dark-dank, furry-purry milk-smelling feline she had been before. She smelled of onions and mustard, pickles and relish. But, as Crow said, she was alive.

"How can we ever thank you?" Marco asked the crow.

"Oh, just keep an eye on your mother and tell me if she's doing poorly," Crow replied.

Geraldine walked in zombielike fashion to the edge of the porch, where she worked her jaws up and down and back and forth to see if she could still speak. Finally she said, "Off."

"What?" asked Timothy.

"She said *off*," replied Polo.

"Off what?" asked Timothy.

"Her body may be alive, but I think her brain is going," said Crow.

Marco, though, understood. "The light goes off, she's saying. Is that it, Mother?"

"Yes," Geraldine said slowly. "When . . . the refrigerator door . . . is closed . . . the light . . . goes . . . off."

While the refrigerator stood open, however, the two tabbies, the crow, and the mouse looked inside and surveyed the contents. Everything seemed to be in a glass jar or a plastic bottle except for the hamburger buns, and the crow decided he needed some kind of nourishment after all his efforts. He had been, after all, deprived of both a mouse and a cat for his breakfast. So he plucked a hamburger bun from the package, left half for Timothy, and flew off with the bottom half of the bun to dip in a nearby birdbath, a crow's equivalent to Dunkin' Donuts.

"Thank you!" Marco and Polo called up to him as the crow soared high above the alley.

"And thank *you*," Polo said to Timothy, closing the refrigerator door by pushing against it. "Once again you've saved a life, little friend."

"Which means you are forever on my 'Do Not Eat' list," Geraldine promised, and that made Timothy very happy indeed.

With their mother between them, Marco and Polo went down the alley to the Fishmonger to find her some breakfast. They came upon a most surprising scene, for the Cat Quartet, having heard the news of Geraldine's sure demise, was already rehearsing a song for the funeral, and the other cats had gathered around to listen:

"Go tell Aunt Rosie,
Go tell Aunt Rosie,
Go tell Aunt Rosie,
The old gray cat is dead.

"Died in the icebox,
Died in the icebox,
Died in the icebox,
Standin' on her head.

"Kittens are cryin',
Kittens are cryin',
Kittens are cryin',
'Cause their mammy's dead.

"Go tell Aunt Rosie
Go . . ."

"Aunt Rosie, my whiskers!" called out Geraldine, her strength returning as she stepped into the circle of cats. "Not so fast, Texas Jake. This old cat may be one cold cat, but I've got a few lives left in me yet; you can count on it."

Texas Jake stared in astonishment at the two tabbies and their mother, but Carlotta rushed over to lick the old cat on the nose. "Oh, Geraldine, I'm so glad!" she meowed. "You did it, and you survived!"

"So tell us, Geraldine," Texas said. "When a refrigerator door is closed, does the light stay on or go off?"

"Off," said Geraldine. "Definitely off. Off, out, zip, zero, zed. When a refrigerator door is closed, it is as dark as a cave inside."

"Hooray!" cried Carlotta again.

"So is she a member of the Club of Mysteries now, Texas?" Polo asked.

Texas Jake wasn't Lord of the Loft, King of the Alley, Commander in Chief, and Cat Supreme for nothing. When graciousness was called for, gracious he was. "Yes," he said, even though he wasn't too happy about it. "Welcome to the Club of Mysteries, Geraldine. You are now entitled to all the perks of membership."

"Whatever," said Geraldine. "Bring on the bacon, please! I'm hungry."

6
A THEOLOGICAL DISCUSSION

If Texas Jake felt he had met his match in Geraldine, he still had Marco and Polo to boss around.

"So!" he said when all the cats had eaten their fill. "Your mother has proven she has spirit, Marco. When do you and your brother plan to bring us the answers to the mysteries *you* were assigned?"

"Spirit, schmirit!" scoffed Geraldine, her pink tongue curling around the rim of her mouth in case any little bit of salmon might have been left behind. "I was just proving to you that you can't get rid of old Geraldine so easily. Now I have a question, Texas Jake. How come *you* get to think up all the mysteries? How come *you* get to send the other cats around on missions that could very well cost them their lives?"

All the cats there in the parking lot looked shocked indeed, for no one had ever asked Texas Jake—Lord of the

Loft, King of the Alley, Commander in Chief, and Cat Supreme—such questions. Even *hearing* the questions made Texas Jake's fur stand on end. Then all the cats began talking at once, telling Geraldine how Texas Jake had fought off Bertram the Bad to save the lives of the club members; how he had gone with Marco and Polo to rescue the smallest of Carlotta's kittens from Steak Knife, the mangy, raggedy leader of the Over-the-Hill Gang, who ruled the dump.

Texas Jake thrust out his chest farther and farther as the stories were told, but Geraldine was unimpressed. "When I see Texas Jake under the hood of a car, or Texas Jake up on a church steeple, *then* I'll be impressed," she muttered. "Until then he's just a big yellow windbag with a bad attitude."

And though Marco and Polo agreed, they were rather glad no one else had heard her, for Texas wouldn't have made it any easier on them if he had! They weren't in any hurry to tackle their assignments. Of course every mystery was talked about long before it was ever solved.

After such a large meal, all the cats wanted to do was go back to the loft and stretch out.

In Murphy's garage again, it was Carlotta who brought up the subject of church steeples. "If you *do* climb up to the very top of one, Polo," she said, lazily licking herself on the old army cot beside the others, "I bet you'll find a nest of gold or silver."

"I don't think so," said Boots. "If the two-leggeds put gold or silver in a nest, a bird might carry it away."

The other cats meowed their agreement. If any cat

other than Carlotta had suggested such a thing, Texas Jake would have said, "A more stupid idea I have never heard!" But because it came from Carlotta, he didn't say a word.

"Maybe our masters put their enemies up there," Elvis ventured. "Maybe they impale them on the sharp points of the steeples and leave them to rot in the sun."

It was such an awful idea that all the cats opened their eyes and stared at him. "Did *you* ever see anything rotting away on a church steeple?" Texas Jake asked.

"No," said Elvis uncertainly.

"Then don't talk nonsense," said Texas Jake, and the loft immediately grew quiet.

Marco was the first to break the silence. He had read something once in the newspaper about churches and cathedrals and temples, and finally he said, somewhat hesitantly, "I believe that steeples are like fingers, pointing the way to God."

All the cats turned to the open window of the loft as though, if they looked out at the sky themselves, they might see this God that Marco was talking about.

"Well, then, enlighten us, Marco, oh cat who can reeeeeeead," said Texas Jake mockingly. "What is this 'God' who lives in the sky?"

"Does he bite?" asked Boots.

"Does he meow?" asked Carlotta.

"Can he fly?" Polo wanted to know.

"Can he swim?" asked Elvis.

"I don't know anything more, except that he is the maker of heaven and earth," said Marco.

The cats put their heads back on their paws and thought some more.

"If that's the case," said Geraldine, "he could have made the nights a little warmer."

"And the wind a little gentler," said Carlotta.

"And the summers a little cooler," said Boots.

Then Elvis asked, "Why do you suppose he made dogs at all?"

"Or river rats?" added Polo.

"God is a mystery," said Texas Jake. "That's why I have asked Polo to climb to the top of a church steeple and solve it for us."

There didn't seem much else to discuss about a God-who-lived-in-the-sky, who had the wisdom to make cats in all their magnificent glory but was foolish enough to make dogs as well. So they all stretched out in their favorite places in the loft, one cat's head on another's belly, one cat's paw over another's ear, tails entangled, paws at rest.

Just as everyone was about to drift off, however, Marco said in a quiet voice, "*God*, read backward, spells *dog*."

All the cats' heads bobbed up.

"Dog?" they meowed in unison.

"What are you saying, Marco?" boomed Texas Jake. "That the God who made heaven and earth is a *dog*?"

"That there's a great labrador retriever up there in the sky?" asked Elvis.

"Or a thoughtful greyhound?" asked Boots.

"Or even a pit bull?" Carlotta shuddered.

"I don't know," said Marco. "It's just an observation."

"That explains why dogs are allowed to bark all night," said Texas Jake.

"And dirty the sidewalks," said Elvis.

"And chase cats," said Polo. "If God is just a great dog in the sky, maybe what the two-leggeds put on top of their steeples is a dog biscuit."

"We'll soon find out, won't we?" Texas Jake said.

And the big yellow cat in the rocking chair put his chin on his paws, his large yellow eyes looking down on Polo. It was a long time before Polo went to sleep, and whenever he awoke from his nap that morning, he thought he could see one of Texas Jake's eyes watching him from above.

Around noon, while the other cats were still napping, Marco and Polo slipped down the stairs and had a little talk out in the alley.

"We don't have to do this, you know," said Marco. "We could just walk away from the Club of Mysteries and never come back. How are you supposed to climb to the top of a steeple, Polo, without breaking your neck and all four legs as well? It's not made out of tree bark, you know."

"And how are you supposed to be hiding under the hood of a car when it starts to purr? The car could grind you up and spit you out, Marco," Polo said.

They hunkered down beside the garbage cans and thought about it.

"If we don't do the mysteries, we will never be able to go back to the club again," Marco said. "We will never be able to enjoy a meal at the Fishmonger without the others mocking us, and Carlotta will not give us a second look."

"And what will our mother think of us if we are too cowardly to try?" Polo said. "*She* was brave enough to get shut inside a refrigerator."

"There's no question; we simply have to do it," Marco said at last. "Unless . . ." His eye fell on Timothy as the little mouse scampered across the alley and behind a garage. "Unless we could get someone else to do it for us."

"Who?" asked Polo.

"What about Timothy?" whispered Marco. "*He* could climb under the hood of a car and escape faster than I could."

Polo was shocked. "You want little Timothy to be ground up by an automobile, Marco? How could you even suggest such a thing?"

"I was afraid you might say that," said Marco.

"On the other hand," said Polo, "why should I risk my life slipping and sliding up a church steeple a hundred feet in the air when Crow, who flies over rooftops every day, could go take a look for me?"

"You have a point," Marco agreed. "Except that, in both your case and mine, the other members of the club will be watching. You don't get points for having somebody else solve a mystery for you."

At that very moment a shadow fell over the alley as two black wings blotted out the noonday sun. Down came Crow, fluttering to a stop ten feet away and walking stiff-legged toward them.

"Did I hear my name?" he cawed.

"Mere speculation," said Marco. "We were discussing a hypothetical situation."

Polo hated it when Marco used big words he couldn't understand.

"A what-if conversation," Marco explained, for Crow did not understand it either.

"And how does a *what* and an *if* concern me?" asked the crow. "How's your mother? A bit more wobbly today, is she?"

"Our mother's fine," said Marco. "But Polo has been given another mystery to solve. He has to find out what it is that humans prize so highly that they would build tall steeples shaped like needles and almost impossible to climb. Surely, Texas Jake figures, the two-leggeds would not construct such impossible structures if they did not plan to hide and protect something very precious there at the very top."

"But you are not suggesting that *I* do your spying for you!" said the crow, feigning a look of shock. "Surely you are not even thinking about cheating."

"Oh, no indeed!" said Polo. "We just mentioned that if there *were* any such thing on the top of a steeple, you, with your sharp eyes, would surely have seen it."

"Yes, I would rather think so," Crow replied, "though I can't honestly say I have looked."

"And I was just suggesting to Polo that for a cat to climb a slippery slope so high in the air might mean his certain death," said Marco.

"Very true, very true," said Crow. "Sad indeed." Polo had the uneasy feeling that even at that very minute, Crow was looking him over, deciding what juicy part of him—if he *should* fall from a steeple—to feast on first.

"Of course, if I had talons I would offer to carry you over the rooftops so you could look down on a steeple and see for yourself," Crow said. "But my claws are not strong enough to hold you, nor my beak, either. I do, however, have an eagle friend who I feel sure would delight in picking up a cat and carrying him high in the air. If you want, I could ask his assistance."

But the cats declined, knowing only too well how eagles were known to drop their prey onto the rocks, and what a feast Crow and his friend Eagle would have if that were to happen to Polo.

"No, thank you," Polo said. "I think I'll take my chance with my own claws on a steeple, if you don't mind."

"Just let me know when you plan to try it, Polo," the crow said, flapping his great wings again for takeoff. "For I would like to be on hand when you make your great climb. And give your mother my regards."

7
The Metal Monster

Even though it was Polo who wanted so desperately to impress his mother, who wanted her to tell him he was special, it was Marco who had the first opportunity to solve his mystery. Geraldine came down out of the loft and crouched down beside him in the alley.

"I have spent many a winter night under the hood of a car, especially a car that has come back from a drive and its insides are still warm," she told him. "Getting up under the hood is no problem, Marco, even for a bag of blubber like you. Just crawl under the car and work your way up its insides until you find a place that's warm and toasty."

"And *then* what?" Marco asked.

"Then . . . I don't know. I always crawled back out again as soon as I heard footsteps and a door slam. By the time the car began to purr, I was gone. I have never been under a hood when a car began to purr."

"But if I stay, I will probably be ground to bits!" Marco protested.

"Well, I have been around longer than you, my son, and I have seen what two-leggeds do sometimes when they park their car on a hill. They take small blocks of wood and put them behind the tires so it cannot roll. All we need to do is nose a couple of blocks of wood behind the wheels of Murphy's car when it is sitting in the garage. Then you climb up under the hood, and when the car begins to purr, you will be inside to see what makes it do that. Mr. Murphy will not be able to go anywhere until he gets out and removes the wood, and when he does, you jump back down."

There were, of course, a few things to consider—first, that Marco was fat. Climbing up into the insides of an automobile's hood was easier for a Timothy mouse or even a Polo than it was for a cat whose great fondness in life was eating.

Second, *because* he was fat, Marco was slow. At least he was not swift. And once the car had begun to purr, Marco knew he'd have to get out before the metal monster began chewing him up.

That evening, after Mr. Murphy came home and parked his car in its usual place, Marco and Polo and their mother snooped about until they found several blocks of wood just the right size in the woodpile. It did not take them long to nose them out of the pile and behind the back wheels of the car.

That done, Marco announced to the rest of the cats that the following morning, when Mr. Murphy came out to go to work, he—Marco—would crawl up under the hood of the car.

It seemed a very brave thing, and Carlotta was most impressed.

"I've never known anyone, Marco, who climbed up under the hood of a car, into the very insides of the beast, and stayed there until the beast woke up," she said. "At last you will be able to tell us what makes an automobile purr."

"It only happens when the driver gets inside," said Boots. "I think he simply sits down and strokes it somehow."

"Or perhaps he gets in and feeds it, and *that's* when it purrs," said Boots.

"Maybe it's the windshield wipers that make it purr. Maybe that's like scratching a cat behind its ears," said Elvis.

"Harrumph!" said Texas Jake, climbing stiffly into the rocking chair and looking down at the little crowd assembled below. "What we *do* know is that the purr doesn't last for more than a few seconds, for then the purr becomes a growl and the growl becomes a roar, and suddenly the huge beast begins to move. Any cat caught inside an automobile at that point—even a cat who can reeeeeeead—is roadkill, to be spat out along the highway like yesterday's trash."

"Oh, Texas, it's too dangerous!" Carlotta cried. "Why are you asking Marco to do that?"

Texas opened his yellow eyes wide. "Did I *tell* him to crawl up under the hood, my dear? No, I did not. I asked him to solve a mystery, and however he decides to solve it is up to him."

Carlotta snuggled against Marco that night and licked him carefully behind his ears and under his chin. Marco began to forget all about the task that lay ahead. He felt he

58

could not be any happier than he was at that moment, lying on his side on the old army cot, Carlotta licking his ears. He tipped his head back farther and farther as her pink tongue lapped at the fur beneath his chin. His eyes closed into tiny slits, and he wondered why church steeples pointed toward the sky. They should point toward Murphy's garage, because there could be no greater paradise than this. What a wonderful world it would be if God had just been a cat, Marco thought. If he had made no dogs at all.

But paradise ended all too soon, for when morning came the cats did not even go to the Fishmonger for breakfast. Instead, as Marco went down the dusty stairs of the loft to the sleeping automobile below, they all arranged themselves on the stairs, like football fans in a stadium.

Marco cast one long look out the door of the garage before he crawled under the car. It was a beautiful morning—a blue-sky, breeze-in-the-wind kind of morning—with spring flowers popping up here and there, too beautiful a morning to be crawling up under the oily insides of an automobile that probably did not like to be wakened any more than Marco did.

"Take your time, Marco," Geraldine called to him from the staircase, where Texas Jake was watching from the very top, like the grand pooh-bah of the realm.

Under the car Marco went. It was dusty. It was dirty. It was greasy and oily and smelly. At first Marco couldn't see any possible way he could get up into the maze of pipes and cables and odd-shaped hunks of metal that formed the inside of the monster's body. But then he saw an opening here, a passageway there—a place to put this paw and a place to put that one—and at last he felt he was as far inside the insides of Murphy's automobile as he could get.

It was not a very comfortable position. One paw was on this thing, one paw was on that, and his belly rested on something flat. But at last he heard the back door of the house open. He heard Mrs. Murphy's usual "Good-bye, Fred." He heard the heavy footsteps of plump Mr. Murphy as he came down the back sidewalk, and then his footsteps sounded there in the garage.

The car door opened and there was the usual huffing and puffing as Mr. Murphy sat down on the seat and maneuvered himself behind the steering wheel. There was a jangle of keys, the same kind of sound Marco heard when Mrs. Neal came back from the grocery store and put her house key in the lock.

All at once the flat thing on which Marco's belly rested gave a snort and a belch, and then . . . then . . . it started to purr! Marco felt that he was lying on the very heart of the metal monster, for its purr grew louder and it became warmer and warmer. Marco knew that if he did not leave immediately he would be one fried cat. Frantically he began backing down off the engine, trying to find the way he had come, but it was far more difficult getting out than it had been getting in, for he had to do everything tail first.

The car did not move, however, though the engine was purring and getting hotter by the minute. Then Marco heard Mr. Murphy say, "What in the world . . . ?" The car door opened once again.

There was more puffing and grunting as Mr. Murphy eased himself out of the automobile, and Marco, in turn, tried to work his way down from under the hood.

As the cats up on the stairs silently watched, Mr. Murphy stooped and looked under his front tires. Then he went back and looked behind his rear tires.

"Now, who in tarnation put these blocks of wood behind my tires?" he fumed. "Who would play a trick like that on me?"

He kicked one block out of the way, then the other. He got back in the car, closed the door, and fastened his seat belt.

But Marco still had not found his way out! He thought it was this way, then he thought it was that. But he did not fit going one way, and his paws slipped the other. The car was starting to move, and the big beast's heart was growing so hot that even though Marco was not touching it any longer, he feared the heat alone would kill him.

"He will be ground up like pepper!" cried Carlotta in terror.

"He's going to be chewed up and spit out the tailpipe!" cried Polo.

"Indeed! Indeed!" said Texas Jake. "Well, so long, my fine fat fellow."

At that moment, Geraldine sprang. She landed on the hood of the car and flattened herself against the windshield, right in front of Mr. Murphy's face. To the man behind the wheel, it looked as though a cat had been sailing through the air and collided with his windshield.

"Jumping Jupiter!" he cried, slamming on the brakes. "What the ding-dong is happening today?"

He blew his horn once to scare off the cat on his windshield. He blew his horn twice. Underneath the hood,

61

the horn sounded like a million trumpets in Marco's tender ears. He lost all sense of balance and direction and found himself tumbling and sliding past pipes and tubes and cables until he landed on the garage floor. Darting out from under the car, he tore up the steps to the loft.

"What is it, Fred?" came Mrs. Murphy's voice from the back porch. "Did you forget your lunch?"

"No, I think I forgot my head today. I seem to have lost my mind," he said. "First the car wouldn't move, and now there's a cat . . ."

But the cat on the windshield was gone.

Mrs. Murphy came into the garage. "What's the matter with you?" she asked.

"Somebody put blocks of wood behind my rear wheels," Mr. Murphy said.

"Then you must have put them there yourself," said his wife.

"I didn't, I tell you! And the next thing I knew, a cat was plastered against my windshield."

Mrs. Murphy looked around. "I don't see hide nor hair of any cat," she said. "I don't think you got enough sleep last night, Fred. Try to have a good day, and I'll see that you get to bed early tonight."

Mrs. Murphy went back into the house, Mr. Murphy and his metal monster rolled out of the garage, and Marco, his paws dirty with grease and oil, looked over at his mother, who had gathered with the other cats beside the rocking chair.

"Thanks, mum," he said.

"What's a mother for?" said Geraldine.

8
DEAD OR ALIVE

Back up on the floor of the loft, all the cats converged on Marco and began helping to clean his fur of grease and oil. All the cats but Texas Jake, that is, who did not care to join in.

Texas Jake had not thought there would be any cat to clean up, and he did not welcome all this attention given to Marco. There was nothing much to do about it, but he intended to show that he was still Lord of the Loft, King of the Alley, Commander in Chief, and Cat Supreme.

"Oh, Marco, you were so *brave!*" purred Carlotta, licking his nose.

"A chip off the old block," said Geraldine, attacking the grease on one of his paws.

"You could have been dog food, and here you are, alive and all in one piece," said Polo happily, licking the oil off the end of his brother's tail.

The fur rose up on the back of Texas Jake's neck. "And *so*, Marco—the cat who can reeeeeeead," he boomed. "Did you or did you not solve the mystery of what makes an automobile purr?"

"I did indeed," said Marco. "It is the same thing that keeps all two-leggeds and four-leggeds alive: a heart. Even metal monsters with four wheels have a heart."

"A heart?" exclaimed the cats in unison.

"It's not the same kind of heart, though I've never seen what my own heart looks like," said Marco. "It is a black metal box, almost as big as you, Texas Jake. And that is what purrs when a car begins to move. In fact, I was lying right on top of the automobile's heart when the purring began, and not only does it purr—a very loud purr, indeed—but the heart becomes hot. *So* hot, in fact, that if I had stayed another minute or two, I would have been one fried feline, I can tell you."

Texas Jake's big, yellow eyes rolled around a time or two before they settled again on Marco. "Ah, but you did not answer the question, Marco!" he scoffed. "You did not solve the mystery! I didn't ask what *part* of the automobile does the purring. I asked what *makes* it purr in the first place." His great yellow eyes narrowed. "What a shame that after all you have been through, you cannot answer that."

"But I can!" said Marco, the hair on *his* neck beginning to bristle. "What makes the heart in a car begin to purr is quite simple, really: a key."

"A key?" cried all the cats.

"I heard it jingle when Mr. Murphy opened the door

of his car. I heard it jangle when he used it again inside the car. And when he turned it, when I heard the click, the huge heart beneath me began to tremble and purr, and my stomach and paws grew warm. A key is your answer, Texas Jake. The mystery is solved. A key is the answer to life."

"Ah!" said all the cats together; all but Texas Jake.

"Then it's a key that makes something come alive!" said Polo, who had to repeat things sometimes in order to understand them.

"Nonsense!" said Texas Jake. "When my master comes home at night, he turns the key in the door, but the house is not alive."

The cats pondered this for a while.

"When my mistress turns the key on her music box, it comes alive," said Carlotta. "Music begins to play, and a little ballerina on top of the box goes around and around."

"Then a key makes *some* things purr and come alive, but not all things," said Marco. "Perhaps if a key makes something *move*, it comes alive. If it does not move, then it just—well, opens a door or something."

"A house, then, is not alive because it does not move," said Texas Jake, wanting the final word on everything. "A music box is alive because it moves."

"But what about skates?" asked Polo suddenly. "Or bicycles? Or wagons? They all move, but they don't have keys."

The cats stared at Polo—they were so surprised that *he* had come up with such a profound observation.

"Yes! Yes!" they began to cry, turning on Marco again.

"How do you explain *that*, Marco?" asked Texas Jake, eager to prove that the cat who could read had not solved his mystery after all.

"Oh, for goodness' sake, Texas Jake, knock it off!" said Geraldine. "You asked him what makes a car purr and he told you. He climbed up into the oily insides of an automobile, he sat on its heart, he singed his paws, he toasted his tail, and he *told* you: A key is what makes a car purr. He doesn't have to explain all the mysteries of life."

That was true, and Texas couldn't deny it. So the cats stood up and stretched, agreeing that some mysteries were imponderable, just too deep for words. And with that they trotted noiselessly down the stairs, heading for the Fishmonger.

Marco had an uneasy thought, however. He remembered seeing gas stations. Seeing cars lined up at gas stations. Seeing big tubes going into cars, feeding them food of some kind—gas, he supposed. Perhaps it was not a key after all that made a car purr, but gas! And then he had a second thought: *He* moved, and *he* wasn't run by a key. But all this he would keep to himself. A key had made Mr. Murphy's car purr that morning, and that was good enough for him.

Of course, at the Fishmonger all the cats wanted to hear the details of Marco's crawling under the hood of the car, and when they had all eaten their fillets of flounder, with a few fries thrown in, the Cat Quartet composed a song in Marco's honor, sung to the tune of "The Battle Hymn of the Republic":

"Our eyes have seen the glory of a wondrous
    cunning cat,
Who has crawled inside an auto and upon its heart
    he sat,
He has felt it start to tremble and it almost fried his fat,
His name goes marching on.
Glory, glory to our Mar-co!
May his life be just a lark-o!
May his days be never dark-o!
His name goes marching on!"

Marco, of course, had never been more pleased, but
Texas Jake was enraged. If *anyone* should have a song sung
in his honor, he thought, it should be him, for *he* was Lord
of the Loft, King of the Alley, Commander in Chief, and
Cat Supreme.

"What's all this 'lark-o' and 'dark-o'?" he hissed. "What
kind of poetry is that? I'll tell you what it is: It's lazy-cat's
poetry. You couldn't find a word to rhyme with 'Marco,' so
you just made one up. A sillier song I never heard!"

"Oh, pipe down, you old windbag," said Geraldine.
"Don't get your whiskers in an uproar just because they're
not singing about you."

Now, no one had ever, *ever* called Texas Jake a windbag
to his face, and Texas Jake was furious. He rose stiffly to his
feet, his back arched, his tail thick, and said, "Madam,
watch what you say, for your days in the Club of Mysteries
are numbered. I have driven away worthier cats than you."

"You have to admit, Texas, that it's not easy finding
words that rhyme with 'Marco,'" the Abyssinian explained.

"But we have heard that you've given Polo an even more difficult mystery to solve: What is at the top of a church steeple? When, and if, Polo manages to solve that mystery, we will compose a song in his honor and do a better job with the rhyming. If he lives, that is. And if he dies . . . ah! The dead have the best songs written about them. Truly they do." He turned his mournful eyes in Polo's direction. "If you slip off the church steeple, Polo, be assured that we here at the Fishmonger will compose a song worthy of all your effort and will be singing your praises for many weeks to come."

I wonder why that doesn't help, Polo thought. He would far rather be down below, with his mother nuzzling his forehead. Yes, he would give up all the songs, all the fuss, and all the glory just to be near his mother for the rest of his life and have her love him best of all. Give up all honor just to be near that soft-warm, dark-dank, furry-purry milk-smelling something he called Mother. Or Geraldine, whichever she preferred.

9
BAD NEWS

Polo felt more and more sad that his mother seemed to prefer Marco to him. She seemed especially impressed that one of her sons could read. If only Polo could do something so splendid that she would remember him always! Perhaps he *would* be able to climb to the top of a steeple. Perhaps he *would* see why the two-leggeds built it so high, what it was they were protecting up there. *Then* his mother would sit up and take notice. *Then* she would tell him what a magnificent cat he was.

When they got back from the Fishmonger, however, her attention was all on Marco. She crawled up on the stack of old newspapers where the tabbies often slept when they stayed overnight in the loft.

"Are these words?" she asked Marco, pointing to the black marks on the white newspaper.

"Yes," said Marco.

"Then read to me," she said. "Tell me what they say."

While the other cats settled themselves on whatever was soft and dry and handy, Marco crouched on the pile of papers and studied the words in front of him. "The Dow Jones average dropped sharply yesterday in response to the quarterly earnings reports. . . ."

"Bor-ing!" said Boots from the old army cot. "Not only is it boring, but hardly a single word makes sense."

Marco looked over the paper and chose something else: "He led the team down the field on their opening drive, just missing two would-be touchdown passes before—"

"Bor-ing!" said Elvis. "Is this what they put in the newspaper, Marco? Why would anyone want to read this stuff?"

"It just depends what section of the newspaper you happen to be reading," Marco said. "Some sections are about money and some are about football and some are about books or food."

"Find a section on food and read that to us," said Geraldine.

So Marco nosed around the pile of newspapers until he found a section with a picture of a fish on the front, a fish with whiskers, and he read, "'Seventeen Ways to Cook a Catfish.'"

All the cats raised their heads and paid attention.

"Is there really such a fish, Marco?" Geraldine asked.

"Yes," Marco told her.

"You know what this means, lads," boomed Texas Jake from the rocker, where he was still grooming himself after his meal. "It's the two-leggeds who give us creatures our names. If there *is* such a fish as a catfish, there will some-

72

day be a cat called a fishcat, and you know what will happen then."

"No," said Carlotta. "What *will* happen, Texas Jake?"

"They'll be eating *us!*" said Texas Jake. "Two-leggeds are always looking for new things to eat: shark fins, buffalo steaks, ostrich eggs, and alligators. It's only a matter of time, I tell you, before there will be all-you-can-eat buffets of fillet of Persian, fried Abyssinian, Siamese salad sandwiches, and tabby chowder."

A shadow fell over the loft just then as Crow appeared in the open window.

"And Crow will be next!" Texas Jake said, to emphasize his point. "Haven't you heard the old saying 'to eat crow'? Mark my words, lads, some day the two-leggeds will be serving cat fillets and breast of crow."

"What are you talking about?" said Crow. "I can fly faster and farther than the two-leggeds could ever imagine. They'd have to catch me first, and no one ever catches Crow."

"So what do you want with us?" Texas Jake asked. "Getting a little hungry, are you? Well, we've got old Geraldine here, but I imagine she's a little too tough even for you."

"Nothing is too tough for Crow, not even you, Texas," cawed the crow. "I wouldn't touch your back or your legs, but your guts and brains would be as tender and succulent as a kitten's, I'll wager."

"Crow, you are disgusting!" cried Carlotta, beginning to weep, for she was thinking of her five little kittens, for whom the Club of Mysteries had found a good home. She hoped that they would never end up a crow's breakfast.

"I have come simply to tell you that the river rats are marauding through the back alleys, so be on guard," Crow replied. "Now that spring is here and humans are no longer filling their bird feeders, pickings are scarce. The vegetables are not yet ripe in the gardens, and fruit has not fallen from the trees. The river rats are hungry. Just a little reminder from your friendly neighborhood crow to be on guard, that's all." He spread his wings again, shoved off, and flew away.

If there was any good in the crow's watchfulness, Polo thought, it was that his keen sense of sight and hearing told them when trouble was on the way.

"I just hope my kittens are safe," said Carlotta. She was thinking of Hamburger, Scamper, Mustard, Sugar, and Catnip, as they were called, who were now living in a nursing home, where the elderly residents loved them.

"They found a good home and I'm sure the doctors and nurses there will keep an extra eye out for them, knowing that rats are around," said Texas Jake.

"I'm more worried about Timothy," said Polo, who had a special fondness for the little mouse.

Still, the river rats gave them something to talk about for the rest of the day. Polo was glad of that, for whenever there was a lull in the conversation, he was afraid that Texas Jake would turn to him and ask, "Well, Polo, of all the church steeples in this town, which one have you decided to climb?"

And indeed, as they made their way to the Fishmonger that evening, Texas did ask.

"I'm thinking," Polo told him. "I'm thinking."

On the way back to the loft after dinner, the cats were

aware of scurryings here and scurryings there. Now and then they saw tiny red eyes glitter and gleam from beneath a trash can lid or a long tail disappear around the corner of a garage.

It was unnerving, even to a cat three times their size, because the river rats were not only extra large, for a common rat, but especially vicious. So when the cats reached the loft, they were all feeling a bit on edge.

"Mother," Polo said timidly, "do you know any bedtime stories you could tell us?"

"Bedtime stories? Bedtime *stories?*" Geraldine said. "Do you think that after raising twenty-nine kittens I have time for stories?"

"I don't know. I'm not too clear on what a mother does. I just thought perhaps you knew some stories," said Polo, disappointed. Maybe he was confusing the two-leggeds with four-leggeds, because whenever the Neals' grandchildren came to visit, Mrs. Neal always knew lots of stories, which she told them at bedtime. Polo, of course, always listened in.

By now, all the cats had chosen their favorite places to sleep, and they were all snuggled down, heads on their paws, watching Geraldine expectantly. Even Texas Jake, from his perch on the rocker, was attentive.

"Well," said Geraldine, who sat upright on the newspapers. "The only stories I ever heard were the stories handed down from my mother and her mother before her. Stories about Old Henna, the Witch Cat."

At this all the heads came up off the paws and all eyes, green and yellow, watched Geraldine in the darkness. For some reason the name seemed familiar.

"Tell us! Tell us!" said Polo.

Geraldine shifted about on her perch of newspapers, then lay down on her side, lapping the last of the flounder from between her claws and giving her coat a lick or two for good measure.

"Well," she said, her green eyes glowing in the dark, "it is said that on nights when there's no moon at all—"

"No moon at all? There's always a moon, even when we can't see it," Marco interrupted.

"Will you shut up?" Boots said. "We're listening to a story."

"—on nights when there is no moon at all," Geraldine continued, with a special look at Marco to make sure he kept quiet, "Old Henna, the Witch Cat, roams the back roads and alleys."

"What does she look like?" asked Carlotta, beginning to shiver.

"Oh, she's a fearsome cat," Geraldine said, "with eyes that shine like silver fish scales and brown fur that glows red at the ends, like coals of fire. And when she walks, her tail slashes *this*away and *that*away, and *this*away and *that*away." Geraldine's tail moved from left to right and right to left. "And when she meows, it's more like a howl, a shriek so shrill that it would send chills up and down your back."

Polo, who was on an old rug, crawled along the floor on his belly a little closer to his mother.

"And it is said in the back roads and alleys," Geraldine continued, "that her breath smells like maggots and her fur stinks like a sewer. Her fur is all matted, her teeth half rotten, and if she comes up to you in the night and breathes

76

on your neck, she can tell by your scent just when you are
likely to die."

Geraldine looked slowly around at the other cats.
"And if it is your time to die, Old Henna will rise up on
her hind legs, her silver eyes will flash, her fur will stand
on end, her tail will thicken, and she will shriek and howl
and shake and wail, so that even creatures three blocks
away will waken, and they too will shiver and shake in the
night."

All the cats seemed to have crept closer together now,
looking about them in the shadows.

77

"Oh, I remember what my mother used to say," Geraldine finished. "If ever I misbehaved, it would be, 'Better watch out, or Old Henna will get you.'"

And suddenly Geraldine rose up on the pile of newspapers, stood on her hind legs, put her front paws in the air, her fur rising, her tail thickening, and gave a horrendous howl, just as one might imagine Old Henna would do.

Every cat in the loft, Texas Jake included, jumped three inches in the air, then cowered in his chosen bed until Geraldine sat down again and began licking her paws.

And somewhere, back in the furthest memories of each of the cats, they seemed to remember hearing someone say the same to them a long time ago, back when they were young. Always, Old Henna was just around the corner, ready to grab them, and it was no surprise that the members of the Club of Mysteries slept closer together that night than they had in a very long time.

10
INTO THE TUNNELS

Sometime in the middle of the night, a cry of a different sort was heard.

The night had been still, except for the far-off barking of a dog and odd scurryings and scuttlings in the alley. The moon, which was waning now, dipped in and out of the clouds, alternately leaving a path of moonlight on the floor of the loft and disappearing again.

Suddenly the air was split by a high-pitched cry of fright and pain that made every cat in the Club of Mysteries lift his head and jump to his feet.

Polo knew in an instant: "Timothy!" he cried.

Not all the cats in the loft believed a mouse worth saving—and some even subscribed to the belief that mice were put on this Earth to be eaten by cats—even *if*, perhaps, the world was created by DOG. Still, every cat, except Geraldine, maybe, remembered that it was the little mouse named Timothy to whom they owed a favor.

Down the stairs of the loft they ran, out the door of Murphy's garage in the moonlight, just in time to see the seven tails of a gang of river rats go streaking down the alley with a little gray mouse dangling from the jaws of the foremost.

"Where are they taking him?" cried Carlotta. "If they're going to eat him, why don't they do it here?"

"He is too tender and succulent a mouse for one rat to eat alone," Texas Jake explained, panting as he ran. "They'll take him down in the sewer and divide him up, for even among rats there's a code of honor."

Down the storm drain at the corner they went. Marco and Polo had been in the sewers before, and they knew which way the water ran and about how far it was to the river. Even if they hadn't, all they needed to do was follow Timothy's pitiful little squeals through the dark tunnels, where the *drip, drip, drip* of water mingled with the *pit-patter-pit* of little rat feet. Red eyes gleamed in the dark pipes that fed into the tunnel.

It was hard to keep up with the rats, however. Texas Jake hadn't even made it down the storm drain, and Carlotta also stayed behind. It was difficult for Marco, but he managed to keep pace with Boots and Elvis. Polo, who was as fast on his feet as he was slow in his mind, was ahead of the pack when he became aware of someone rapidly moving up on his left, soon to overtake him. He discovered it was his mother. She may have been an old cat, and she may have had twenty-nine kittens, but she was a fast alley cat, used to fending for herself. Her muscles were toned, her flesh was lean, and she proved as good a runner as any.

Like a horse at the races, she was breathing harder and harder, her breath coming in little puffs, and then she gave a sudden mighty leap. A terrible squeal echoed from one end of the tunnels to the other.

The pack of rats came to a stop when they heard the cry, for Geraldine had captured not the rat carrying Timothy but their leader. A moment later she wheeled about and raced back the way they had come, the head rat in her jaws.

Now the rat pack truly did not know what to do, for there could be no killing and dividing and eating of the succulent mouse in the jaws of one without an order from their leader. And because their leader was now being carried back *up* the alley, away from the river, the rat pack had no choice but to turn on their little rat feet and follow along.

A patch of light appeared up ahead as the cats and the rats reached the opening to the street. And there Texas Jake was waiting for them. In his big, booming voice, Marco and Polo heard him say, "Well, what have we here—the rattiest of the nastiest of the rat pack himself? The esteemed leader?"

Crawling out of the tunnel onto the sidewalk above, the rats and the cats faced off, and when Geraldine, her mouth foamy with her own saliva, dropped the rat leader on the cement, the other cats pounced and held him down with their claws.

"It seems we have a little trade to make," Texas Jake said to the rats. "One tiny, succulent mouse by the name of Timothy for one nasty, flea-bitten, miserable rat. What do you say, boys? Will you make the trade?"

The rat pack didn't answer, looking toward their leader for instruction.

"Let . . . him . . . go," the rat leader choked, Marco's paw a little too close to his throat.

And so the rat who was holding Timothy in his jaws let him go, and immediately Timothy sprang toward Polo for protection. At the same time, the cats let the rat leader go, and he scurried back down into the sewer with the pack.

The trade was made just as morning began to dawn over the street and the first few birdcalls broke the stillness. As the tired cats moved back down the alley, shielding little Timothy with their bodies, they heard the rats chanting behind them:

> "Trail them,
> Tail them,
> Sniff them,
> Whiff them.
> Dodge them,
> Lodge them,
> Trip them,
> Tip them.
> Poke them,
> Smoke them,
> Steer them,
> Shear them. . . ."

For now, however, the river rats were obliged to settle for getting their boss back, not breakfast. Of course they would be more eager than ever to get revenge on the cats, but for the moment, at least, there was peace of sorts in the alley.

"Geraldine," said Carlotta, "that was a brave and noble thing you did. Timothy once warned us that my little kitten Catnip had been catnapped, and that helped us get him back. No one could be happier than I am that Timothy is safe."

"*I'm* happier!" said Timothy, trying out his squeak to see if it still worked. "I am even happier than you are, Carlotta; I thought for sure I was a goner. A goner and a breakfast both. I can't thank you enough, Geraldine."

"I can see that until the vegetables are ready in the fields and fruit is ripe on the trees, we will probably be sharing our dinners at the Fishmonger with the rats now and then," Texas Jake said. "But for now, I suggest we go celebrate."

There always seemed to be something to celebrate, and the Fishmonger was a favorite place to do it. When the story got out of how little Timothy had been saved because Geraldine had captured the leader of the rat pack, the Cat Quartet decided to compose a song in her honor. When you're a cat, there's always a reason to eat, a reason to sleep, and a reason to meow. And so Elvis, the Persian, the Abyssinian, and the Siamese crawled up on the wall at the end of the parking lot and sang a song to Geraldine:

> "We . . . want a cat,
> Just . . . like the cat
> That married dear old dad.
> She . . . was a cat,
> And . . . the best-est cat
> That Daddy ever had.
> A good old-fashioned cat

84

With heart so true,
She'd catch a rat to save
A mouse or two, so
We . . . want a cat,
Just . . . like the cat
That married dear old dad."

Oh, it was a lovely morning. A festive morning. A delightfully warm and springlike morning, but somehow Polo felt uneasy.

Whenever he looked in Texas Jake's direction, Texas seemed to be looking at him. As he snuggled up to his mother in the parking lot, he saw Texas Jake's eyes flash and his tail twitch, and Polo knew, as sure as he had four paws, that Texas Jake wouldn't wait much longer for him to solve the mystery of what the two-leggeds put at the very top of a church steeple.

And to Polo it seemed as though his days were numbered, his time on Earth was nearly done, and very soon, within the next day or so, possibly even tomorrow, he would have to choose a church and climb the steeple.

11
GOOD AND EVIL

Sure enough, when the cats got back to the loft, Texas Jake remarked that in another two weeks or so, the moon would be down to a mere sliver. By the time it was full again, Polo would not be welcome back into the club as a member in good standing—unless, of course, he happened to solve the mystery of what the two-leggeds keep at the top of their steeples.

Polo longed to be relieved of this mystery. But even more than that, he wanted some special time with his mother. He wanted nothing more than to follow her about and bask in her scent and snuggle against her fur and let her lick his forehead. He wanted nothing more, that is, except to make her proud of him.

But all she'd said when they had found each other was "Must be one of mine," as she'd sniffed him. Polo needed more than that. He had not been yearning all this time for his mother just for that.

Elvis asked Geraldine where she had been all these years.

"Here, there, and everywhere," Geraldine replied. "I have been to the pound twice and adopted by little old ladies in need of a cat; I have been known to sit on a stranger's porch and meow till they let me in. I have stowed away on a sight-seeing boat and cruised down the river. I have been given away, sold, traded, and fallen in the river once and almost drowned. I have been put in a bicycle basket by a ten-year-old maniac and ridden half-crazed around a neighborhood, but I have survived, and here I am. Wouldn't be surprised if I had a couple more batches of kittens before my time is up."

"You must have seen all kinds of two-leggeds," said Carlotta. "Good and bad, polite and cruel . . . There is a great difference among them."

"Like the difference between food and garbage," said Geraldine.

"What do you think it is," Boots asked, "that makes some two-leggeds kind and some two-leggeds cruel? My master, for example, is kind and thoughtful, but his girlfriend is perfectly dreadful to me. As long as my master is watching, she smiles and pets me, but as soon as he leaves the room, she pushes me off her lap. She brushes my hair off her skirt and covers her nose when she passes my litter box."

The cats all nodded their heads, for they knew just what he was talking about.

"I got even with her, though," said Boots. "One evening when my master left the room, his girlfriend pushed me off the couch—wouldn't even let me sit beside her. So I hopped up on the chair where she had left her angora sweater, and

I hacked up a huge hair ball right onto one of the sleeves."

All the cats meowed their approval.

"What happened then?" asked Elvis.

"I heard a scream, and I was out of there," Boots told him. "So why are some two-leggeds good and others bad?" he asked again. "I've never figured it out."

"I think it's something they eat," said Polo. "I think that people who are mean to cats have a sour stomach. Too much lemon pie, perhaps."

"I think their shoes are too tight," said Geraldine.

"If you want *my* opinion—" began Elvis.

"We don't," said Boots, but Elvis gave it anyway.

"*I* think," he said, "that two-leggeds are mean if they can't sing. What are vocal cords for, I ask you, if not to make song? Show me a person who doesn't sing and I will show you a grump."

The big yellow cat in the rocking chair turned his large head in Marco's direction and said, "Well, the other idiots have been heard from, Marco. What do *you* think, oh cat who can reeeeeeead?"

Marco thought about some of the articles he had read in the papers at the bottom of his litter box. Then he said softly, "Well, perhaps a two-legged who is mean is a person who had some meanness done to him at one time or another, so he's cruel to others in turn."

"*Wrong! Wrong! Wrong!*" cried Texas Jake, slashing his tail back and forth in the rocker. "A more ridiculous reason I never heard."

"Then what *is* the reason that some two-leggeds are cruel, Texas Jake?" asked Carlotta.

"It all has to do with the shape of their necks," the big cat said.

"Their necks?" said Marco, surprised.

"Their necks, lad. Answer this question, if you will: What sinks? That which is up or that which is down?"

"Well, if something is already down, I guess it can't sink any lower," said Marco. "The answer, then, is that which is up."

"Correct, oh brilliant cat who can reeeeeeead," said Texas Jake. "It stands to reason that a two-legged, being the only animal that walks on its hind feet, will find, over time, that his brains are sinking. Little by little, day by day, month by month, they are leaking out of his head, down through his neck and into his feet. It stands to reason, does it not, that the widest necks will allow the most brain matter to get through, and the narrowest necks will let it leak through only a little at a time. This is your answer, then. The neck, lads, the neck. Those with thick necks lack brains and are cruel. Those with skinny necks have a few brains left and are kind."

Geraldine, who had been sleepily resting her head on her paws, turned around and looked at the big yellow cat speaking so pompously from his place in the rocking chair.

"Texas, you are so full of beans they are coming out of your ears," she said. "You seem to be saying that if all two-leggeds lived long enough, their brains would be in their toes, simply because they walk upright."

"That's true," Texas huffed.

"Then why are some *four*-leggeds as mean as they come? How did the river rats, or Steak Knife and his gang,

89

get to be so awful? Not to mention that horrible dog down the alley, Bertram the Bad?"

"Ah!" said Texas Jake. "That's a mystery. Just another mystery of life that needs solving, Geraldine."

"The mystery *I* would like solved is how you came to be Lord of the Loft, King of the Alley, Commander in Chief, and Cat Supreme of this outfit," said Geraldine. "If anyone's brains are in their feet, I'd say they were yours, if you had brains up there to begin with."

Polo was horrified to hear her talk so. "Mother, don't!" he mewed, knowing that Texas Jake would only take his anger out on him if Geraldine vexed him too much. But it was too late.

"Woman," boomed Texas Jake, "your days here at the club are numbered. Watch your tongue."

The cats were shocked into silence. To call another cat "woman" or "man" was about the worst insult possible. To imply that a cat was no more worthy than a two-legged was as bad as calling a cat a dog.

Even Geraldine said no more after that. But that evening, just as Polo had predicted, Texas Jake turned his anger on him.

"Well, Polo," he said. "From the look of the moon and the clouds, I would guess that tomorrow would be a purrfect day for climbing a church steeple, don't you think? For we *all* want to know what it is that the two-leggeds keep up there so high in the air. Yes, my lads, only the birds can possibly know what it is, and Polo here is going to find out."

12
STEEPLE CHASE

Polo was out walking the streets in the early morning before full light, looking at churches and steeples. He was trying to decide which steeple was the lowest and maybe the easiest to climb, but he wasn't having much luck. All of the steeples seemed impossibly high to him. All seemed impossibly steep. In other words, all of them seemed impossible.

Some had a cross on top. Some had a gilded ball. Some had a star, some had a moon—there were shapes of every sort. And some had nothing at all, just a sharp point directed toward the sky.

It wasn't a perfect day, either, for the sky was gray and the air was damp. At last, because he must, Polo made a decision. He chose a church that had a shingled steeple. At the very top of the steeple was a flat square, about the size of a book, and on top of the square was a ball.

He had thought he would go back to the loft and at least enjoy one last breakfast with the others at the Fishmonger. But the more he thought about it, the more he believed that perhaps a cat with an empty stomach had a better chance of climbing the steeple than one full of bacon and biscuits. Besides, if he fell off and died a disgraceful death, he did not want Carlotta or his mother watching.

And so, with no good-bye to anyone, Polo walked around the church, surveying it from every angle. At last he climbed a sycamore tree that grew next to it. Up the trunk he went to the first branch, past that branch to the second, up past the third and fourth, until at last he was even with the roof.

There he was, walking across the shingled roof in the gray May dawn.

At the very tip top of the roof, in the middle of the spine, in fact, was the shingled steeple, and looking up, Polo thought it seemed far taller, far steeper, far more dangerous and impossible than it had ever seemed from the ground.

Nevertheless, he tested his claws on the shingles and they seem to hold, so he began to climb . . . slowly . . . carefully . . . laboriously. First the right front paw, then the left rear foot, then the left front paw, then the right rear foot.

At that moment, the other cats spotted Polo, and it wasn't long before all the cats on their way to the Fishmonger had gathered below. The Cat Quartet, of course, immediately composed a song to spur him on:

"Off he goes, into the wild blue yonder,
Climbing high, into the sun.
There he goes, maybe he's gone forever,
Atta boy, give 'er a run.
If he falls, we're going to miss our Polo.
Things won't . . . seem quite the same.
He'll reach the top,
Or land ker-plop.
Polo is sure to bring our town fame."

Even from this distance, Polo could hear the growl in Texas Jake's chest. Perhaps it was only that it was early morning and the streets were unusually quiet, and it was just his tummy growling. But it seemed obvious to Polo that the big cat had never even expected Polo to try and was not happy about the song sung in his honor.

At the sound of the growl, Polo made the mistake of looking down, and the ground had never seemed so far below as it did just then. For a moment he almost lost his footing, but when he caught sight of his mother and Carlotta watching anxiously from below, he dug in his claws once more, lifted his eyes to the sky, and went on.

A shadow fell over him just then, and Polo saw the wings of the crow as it circled him there on the steeple.

"Good morning, good morning, good morning!" the crow cawed, dipping his wings in salute as he soared this way and that. "So you decided to try your stunt before breakfast, I see."

"It's not *my* stunt. Texas Jake thought it up," Polo replied.

He was not sure whether he found Crow's presence to be comforting or not. "I thought *you* would be at breakfast."

"Oh, I haven't decided on the menu yet," the crow said. "I'm just waiting, you might say, to see what develops."

He could hardly have put it more crudely, Polo thought. What Crow was waiting for, of course, was to see whether Polo ended up on the pavement below.

"I like my breakfasts warm," the crow continued. "And a quick tour of the neighborhood tells me that there is no warm breakfast in sight. Yet."

Polo's paws were beginning to hurt because he had dug his claws so deeply into the shingles.

"Crow," he said, "you have flown over all these steeples hundreds of times. Can't you just land up there on the very top and tell me what's there? Is the ball made of silver or gold or something?"

"Why, Polo, I'm surprised at you! Indeed I am," said Crow. "This is *your* test. If I were to tell you, there wouldn't be much point in your being up here, now would there?"

"I guess not," Polo panted. "But can you just tell me how close I am to the top? I can't even see the book and the ball or whatever they are from here."

"Just keep working at it," said the large bird. "Don't worry about how far you are from the top. And if you get tired, just let go and slide right back to the roof."

"Slide back to the roof?" exclaimed Polo. "If I let go for an instant, I probably wouldn't stop at the roof. I'd slide right down to the pavement."

"Whatever," said the Crow. "But don't let me distract you."

"Don't you ever think of anything but what you're going to eat next?" Polo asked.

"Easy for *you* to say," said Crow. "All you have to do to get a warm meal is return to the people who take you in and care for you. Your little jaunts to Murphy's garage and the Fishmonger are just short excursions to you. But every bite of food I put in my mouth I have to drum up myself. So climb up or slide down, Polo. Either way, I will honor and appreciate you, especially with a little salt and pepper on the side."

Down below, Marco was getting nervous. It bothered him to see Polo up there all alone. But Marco knew he would be useless up on the steeple himself. His brother might be stupid sometimes, but he was swift and agile, and if anyone could climb a steeple, it was Polo.

Geraldine, too, paced nervously on the sidewalk, her green eyes turned up toward the steeple. And then . . . then it began to rain. It wasn't a thunderstorm with bolts of lightning, just a spring shower. But even from down below, Marco and his mother could tell that the rain was making the shingles slippery. It seemed that for every three inches Polo progressed up the steeple, he slid back five.

But finally . . . finally . . . Polo reached the top. There was a hush on the sidewalk below as his fellow cats watched him place one paw over the flat block that looked like a book, then another. Finally, there was Polo at the top of the steeple, his front paws wrapped around the ball, his rear feet on the book.

High in the air, he hung on for dear life while the crow circled. And there at the top of the steeple, Polo made a

terrible discovery: It looked a lot more scary going down than it had coming up. Not only that, but the roof and the steeple were in need of repair. Some of the shingles were loose and jiggled and slid under his paws. What's more, the book and the ball were loose and wobbled back and forth beneath his weight.

"Meow!" Polo wailed as he wobbled from one side to the other. And then *"Meow!"* again, more loudly.

"Oh, Polo!" cried Carlotta from below.

Polo looked down at the lovely Carlotta standing there in the rain, looking up with her large eyes fastened anxiously on him, and wondered if he would live to nuzzle her again. He was too frightened to let go for an instant and could not imagine how he had gotten that high, nor could he even think of trying to climb down.

"Meow!" he cried again, even more plaintively.

And then he heard an answering "Meow" from somewhere down below. He scanned the crowd and saw Carlotta and Marco, Boots and Elvis and Texas Jake and the members of the Cat Quartet, but he could not see his mother.

Again he heard an answering "Meow" from somewhere. Turning his head, he saw Geraldine across the street from the church, sitting in front of the doors to a city fire station.

"Meow!" she called again, as only a mother can meow.

A side door opened and a fireman stepped out. "Hey, cat, you've got a siren on you that could wake the dead," he said. "What's the matter? You hungry?"

"Meow!" Geraldine cried again.

The fireman went back inside and returned with a slice

of salami. He broke it into little pieces and threw them on the ground in front of Geraldine. "Eat up," he said. "Come on, kitty. The rain's stopped. Get your breakfast while you can."

But Geraldine only backed away and meowed all the harder.

A woman who happened to be walking by paused to watch the little drama in front of the fire station, but across the street, two men stood with their necks craned upward. One pointed toward the steeple, and the fireman noticed.

"Hey, what have we got here?" he said. And then, looking up, "Well, I'll be durned. Now just what makes a cat crawl up a steeple, I'd like to know."

The woman looked up too, as more people gathered. And from the top of the slippery church steeple, Polo saw the doors of the firehouse suddenly open. He saw an engine roll out. He saw it cross the street and stop in front of the church. And then he saw the big metal monster begin to stretch. Up and up and up went its neck.

Polo was more frightened than ever, because he thought it was coming to knock him down. But the next thing he knew, a two-legged was climbing up the neck of the beast, hand over hand, until he was as high as Polo. Then the long metal neck swung around and the fireman leaned over and put out one hand.

"Here, kitty-kitty-kitty," he called. "Don't you scratch me, now."

As much as Polo hated to be called kitty-kitty-kitty, he felt quite sure that the two-legged meant him no harm and had come to help. So when the fireman leaned closer, Polo let go and fastened himself like Velcro to the fireman's sleeve instead.

There they were, coming down the neck of the red metal monster while the small crowd on the sidewalk cheered. A minute later the fireman set Polo on the ground beside his mother.

"There you go, ma'am," the two-legged said. "This little guy's safe now. Tell him to stay off steeples, will you?"

The big red monster pulled its neck back down and folded it up under its wing, one of the strangest sights Polo had ever seen. And then came the moment Polo had been waiting for all his life, perhaps: Geraldine licked him up one side of his head and down the other. Purring loudly, he let her clean his ears and lick his nose, and he would have been happy to stand there on the sidewalk forever just to let his mother wash him.

But Texas Jake was hungry and did not see any sense in waiting until Polo was thoroughly clean and dry.

"To the Fishmonger!" he cried, and they all set off down the alley. "Well, Geraldine," he said as they walked along. "It seems that one of your twenty-nine kittens can reeeeeeead, and the other isn't smart enough to climb back down the way he went up. Now what do you make of that?"

"All I know is that he was brave enough to go up there in the first place, and that's more than you can do, you big bag of Texas bones," scolded Geraldine. "He's done what you asked, so now let him be. He's a member in good standing once again, though why he would *want* to belong to this club is a mystery to me."

"Ah, indeed!" said Texas Jake, rolling his big yellow

eyes. "But he hasn't answered the question, Geraldine. I did not tell him to climb the steeple. How he got up there is no concern of mine. The question was, what is it that the two-leggeds put up there so high? That was the mystery he was to solve. And from the look of things, I would guess that once he got up there, Polo was too frightened to notice." He turned his eyes on Polo, and all the cats waited. "And so, Polo, what do they hide at the top of a church steeple? Gold? Silver? A salmon fillet smothered in dill sauce or a big ball of catnip? What did you find at the very tip top?"

Polo looked at the big cat. "Pigeon poop," he said.

All the cats reared back in astonishment.

"What?" cried Texas Jake. "You crawled all the way up there to tell me that all the two-leggeds put there is poop?"

"The two-leggeds don't put it there, the pigeons do," said Polo. "There is nothing more to tell you. Some steeples have crosses, some have stars, some have half moons or balls or books or any manner of object on top of them. Some have no object at all. But I can assure you, they all are visited at one time or another by pigeons."

Crow was flying overhead, and he swooped down to join the conversation. "He's right, Texas Jake," he cawed. "There is nothing up there of any value."

"Then why do the two-leggeds build them so sharp and steep, making them so hard to climb?" Texas wanted to know.

"I've told you, Texas," Marco put in. "Steeples are fingers pointing to God. They are simply designed to take the two-leggeds' minds off things of this Earth so they can ponder the mysteries of life."

101

Texas Jake thought about this for some time, and finally he said, "And all they would have to do is join our club, for that is our purpose too, is it not, lads and lasses? To solve the mysteries of life? I believe we're one step ahead of the two-leggeds after all."

Of course, the Cat Quartet was ready with a song in Polo's honor, sung to the same tune as the song they had composed for Marco:

"Our eyes have seen the glory of a cat high in the air.
He was dangling from a steeple, he was hanging by a hair.
He was there to solve a mystery, though in truth we didn't care.
His name goes marching on.
Glory, glory to our Po-lo,
He was forced to climb it so-lo,
Raise a cup of steaming co-coa,
His name goes marching on!"

It was a moment Polo would never forget. *He* was being honored. It was *his* name being sung. He had proved himself worthy of a lick or two from an adoring mother. Yet it was his mother who had gotten him down. If it hadn't been for Geraldine, he might even now be splattered on the pavement.

Was there ever a day that had turned out better than this one? Polo thought as he retrieved a piece of perch from the garbage can and began to eat. Had things ever gone as well?

But a great shock awaited the cats when they returned to Murphy's garage, for it looked as though a tornado had ripped through the loft.

The moth-eaten fur coat that had made a nice bed in the past was halfway down the stairs; the pile of newspapers had been chewed and scattered; old galoshes, socks and raincoats had been tossed about the loft like leaves. A hat rack was tipped over, flowerpots overturned, and all the clothes in the rag box had been flung about like the petals of a flower, blown to the four winds.

13
TROUBLE

The cats knew immediately what had happened in their absence because they could smell his scent. It was Bertram the Bad, the huge mastiff who lived a few blocks away and who hated cats almost more than he hated his leash. He had somehow got away from his master on their morning walk and, knowing that this was the club hangout, had rushed up the stairs hoping to tear a few cats to pieces. The cats all being gone, however, he'd torn up the place instead.

At that very moment they heard Mr. Murphy come outside to get in his car. When he saw the old fur coat on the stairs he gave a yell, and his wife came out of the house.

"I'll bet those darned cats have been up in the loft again," he said. "Just look what they've done now!"

"That does it!" said his wife. "We've got to get rid of them, Henry. You need to buy a door to that loft and keep it closed. I've a good notion to call the pound and tell them to come cart the whole kit and kaboodle away."

Up the stairs the Murphys came, dragging the fur coat with them. The cats froze as though someone had turned them into statues, as if to prove they were incapable of such mayhem. But Mr. Murphy picked up a broom and his wife grabbed a mop. They went whooshing and whacking around the place until every cat had been chased down the steps and scattered every which way.

But the members of the Club of Mysteries regrouped again that afternoon at the Fishmonger. After they had eaten their fill, they held a meeting by the back wall.

"Lads, we have a problem," said Texas Jake as the cats maintained a respectful silence. If anyone knew what to do, it was Texas. "The two-leggeds think that we have vandalized the loft, and there's no way we can tell them it was Bertram, not us."

"True, true!" agreed the cats.

"The Murphys' loft has been like home to us for several years, and we aren't likely to find another place as convenient," Texas Jake went on. "We've got to put our heads together. We've got to scramble our brains and think of a way out of this. If Murphy puts a door at the top of the stairs, we're done for. What I need now is ideas."

All the cats tried to think harder than they had ever thought before.

"Ideas?" Texas Jake said again. "Anybody?"

"I could go up to Mr. Murphy and purr and brush against his leg," said Carlotta.

"And get cat hair all over his pants? I don't think so," said Texas.

"We could crawl in through the loft window if he puts a door at the top of the stairs," said Polo.

"You have wings, I presume?" said Texas. "*Intelligent* ideas, anybody?"

"We could poison Bertram and take over his doghouse," said Boots.

Texas Jake only rolled his eyes in disgust. "Elvis?" he asked.

"Perhaps we could serenade the Murphys under their window," Elvis said.

"Not only would they chase us out of the garage, they would chase us out of the neighborhood," said Texas. "Geraldine? What have you to suggest? Or Marco, the cat who can reeeeeeead?"

"Somehow we have to get the Murphys to change their minds," said Marco.

"Obviously, my good fellow. *Obviously*. One does not have to know how to read to figure *that* out."

"*I* can help," said a small voice, and everyone looked at Geraldine, for she was the only one who had not spoken yet. But it was not Geraldine at all. It was Timothy.

"You? How can *you* help?" Texas Jake asked.

"I would like to show my appreciation for your saving my life," Timothy squeaked. "Tell me this: What do the two-leggeds hate even more than cats in their garages?"

"Mice in their houses," said Texas Jake.

"Correct!" said Timothy. "Now just suppose that I were to get all my brothers and sisters and cousins and grandparents and aunts and uncles and all the neighborhood mice from miles around to descend on Murphy's garage.

106

My friends, the Murphys would be begging you to come back. And as soon as they did, we mice would disappear."

"Is that a promise?" asked Texas Jake.

"If you will promise in return that none of us will be eaten. For we will have with us baby mice and sister and brother mice and ancient great-grandfather mice—mice of every description. And unless I have your sacred word that they will not be harmed in any way, I can't invite them here."

"Go! Go! Go! You have my word as Lord of the Loft, King of the Alley, Commander in Chief, and Cat Supreme that we won't harm so much as a whisker on your fat little heads," Texas Jake said.

So off Timothy went, and in a matter of hours there was a soft pitter-patter of feet. Dozens of feet. Hundreds of feet. There was a blanket of mice over the Murphys' back yard—an army of mice.

When Mr. Murphy drove his metal monster back home that evening, he braked to a stop right in the middle of the alley and did not even try to turn into his driveway. For there in his yard were hundreds of mice, covering the ground like snow. All he could do was sit in the car and honk his horn. When his wife came out to see what was wrong, she gave a scream. She made her way out to the garage and found mice covering every square inch of floor space. Mice were sitting on a spare tire, swinging on a light chain, dancing on the workbench, gnawing through a wall, squeaking and squealing hither and thither. She turned toward her husband, who was still trapped in his car in the alley. Mice were crawling around on top of it, sliding down

the windshield, peeking over the license plates, running along the bumpers, and the air was filled with the high-pitched squeak of a thousand mousy voices.

"The cats! We need the cats!" screamed Mrs. Murphy. "Oh, why did we ever chase them away?"

"Nothing they did was ever as bad as all these mice!" cried her husband. "It's an infestation! An invasion!"

"There's only one thing to do. We must bring the cats back," said his wife. "I'll go open some tuna fish."

As all seven members of the Club of Mysteries watched from behind the garbage cans, Mrs. Murphy went back inside the house and came out again with several opened cans of tuna fish. Her husband got out of the car, a mouse dangling from the rim of his hat. Stepping between clusters of mice, the Murphys placed the cans on the first step of the loft, then went to the back gate and, turning to the east, called, "Kitty-kitty-kitty!" They turned to the west. "Kitty-kitty-kitty!" The south. "Kitty-kitty-kitty." The north.

"Aren't they ridiculous?" Geraldine whispered to Carlotta. "What self-respecting mother would ever name her kitten 'kitty-kitty-kitty'?"

"Please come back!" Mrs. Murphy pleaded.

"All is forgiven," Mr. Murphy begged.

"You can have my old fur coat. You can sleep in the rag box. Just come chase these awful mice away," called Mrs. Murphy.

Finally Mr. Murphy carefully drove his car into the garage, and the Murphys went back in the house, closing the door securely behind them.

109

"Well done, Timothy," said Marco.

"You have won the loft for us again, and we shall protect you and your children and your children's children for as long as the Club of Mysteries goes on," said Texas Jake.

"Thank you," said Timothy. And at his command, all his mouse sisters and brothers and cousins and aunts and uncles and grandparents . . . all the baby mice and the ancient great-grandfather mice went back to their homes, and soon the Murphys' driveway and garage was as clear of mice as it had been before.

The cats devoured the tuna fish, nosing the cans right off the step when every little bit had been eaten. Then they went back up to the loft and settled down in their usual places—one on the old fur coat, one in the rag box, one in a large boot, two on the army cot, one on what remained of the pile of newspapers, and Texas Jake in the rocker.

"I guess that almost does it for this month. We have no further business, am I right?" Texas Jake asked the others.

"Wrong," said a voice.

"Who said that?" asked Texas, looking around.

"I did," said Geraldine. "I have further business. I want to have a little talk with Bertram the Bad."

"You're out of your mind," said Texas Jake. "Bertram doesn't talk. He only barks. He has rocks in his head where his brains should be."

"Nevertheless, it's time for a talk," said Geraldine. "But we'll put that off till tomorrow. We have had enough excitement, I think, for one day."

14

A LITTLE TALK WITH BERTRAM

The next morning Geraldine set out to have her little talk with Bertram, and the entire Club of Mysteries wanted to go along. Texas Jake, of course, had a smile a mile wide on his face, so sure was he that the tabbies' mother would be devoured by the huge dog.

"May I suggest," he said, "that you hop right down there in the yard with him, Geraldine, and talk to him face to face."

"You'd like that, wouldn't you, old whiskers-face?" said Geraldine. "Well, I didn't raise twenty-nine kittens for nothing. I learned a *little* something along the way."

With that, she put her tail high in the air and led the procession down the alley. When they got near Bertram's yard, she said, "Now, I don't intend to have you sitting up there on the fence with me. If you want to listen in, you can go to that toolshed over there and sit on the roof. But I don't want a sound out of you." She looked around at the rest of the cats. "*Any* of you! This is between Bertram and me."

The cats did as they were told. It took Texas Jake a few moments to hop from a trash can to a fence to the roof of the toolshed because of his slightly lame leg, and it took Marco even longer because of his fat. But there they were.

When they were all quietly seated some distance away, Geraldine walked along the fence until she came to the big animal's doghouse. She crouched down on the fence right behind it, watching the big paw that extended out the door and listening to the huge mastiff snore.

"Bertram!" she called sternly. "Come out of there! I'd like to have a little talk with you."

The snoring from inside ceased at once, and there was a sound like huge jaws suddenly snapping together. The ground began to shake, the doghouse began to tremble, and suddenly from out of the door came the big dog, snarling and barking and carrying on.

"Oh, pipe down!" said Geraldine. The dog paused only momentarily at this strange command and then went into a frenzy, running around and around the perimeter of the fenced yard as though he were half crazed.

Each time he came to the spot underneath where Geraldine was sitting, he leaped up, trying to rattle the fence and knock her off. But Geraldine only clung all the harder to the wood posts. The fence was too high for Bertram to reach her.

She simply looked the other way, studied the birds in the trees, the clouds in the sky.

When Bertram finally stopped for a moment, exhausted,

to catch his breath, she asked, "Now, aren't you ashamed of yourself?"

It had been so many years since Bertram the Bad had heard anyone say that to him, so many years since he'd been a young pup being raised by his mother and grandmother, that he stood stone still and stared at her.

"*Look* at you!" Geraldine continued. "You are enormous! You have strong and powerful jaws. Your paws are as big as melons and your teeth as sharp as an ax. You could tear a cat in two in the blink of an eye, so what are you trying to prove?"

Bertram could only stare in astonishment. The cats over on the roof of the toolshed stared too.

"What makes you feel so weak and inferior?" Geraldine went on.

"What?" roared Bertram. "Weak? Inferior? *Me?*"

"Yes, you. Why would a dog as powerful as you have to act so ferocious? *We* know how terrible you can be. Who are you trying to convince?"

"I'm big, I'm bad, and I'm powerful," brayed Bertram, roaring even louder.

"We know," said Geraldine.

"I can tear you limb from limb," said Bertram.

"We know that, too."

"I am King of the Neighborhood. Everyone fears me. Everyone knows how mighty I am."

"Except you," said Geraldine. "If *you* knew how powerful you are, you could afford to be more gentle. You could use your mighty strength to protect others instead of trying to terrify little kittens."

Marco and Polo watched in admiration, for Bertram's tail began to lower until it was between his hind legs, and his massive head began to droop.

"Just why *do* you carry on so, Bertram?" Geraldine asked, more softly.

Bertram lay down on his belly and put his head on his paws. None of the cats in the Club of Mysteries had ever seen such a thing in their lives.

"I guess it's the yard," said Bertram.

"The yard?" asked Geraldine.

"Yes. Look at my legs. Look at my paws. Look at my massive body. I was meant for running, for jumping, for leaping, for chasing, for bounding up over hills and valleys and leaping over streams. Instead, this yard is my prison, and the only way I can get any exercise is to run madly around in circles."

"I see," said Geraldine.

"Now, think what would happen if every morning I got up and went racing around my yard in circles for no reason at all that my owners could see. Why, they would take me to the vet faster than you could flick your tail. They would probably take me to an animal psychiatrist."

"What's that?" asked Geraldine.

"A doctor who figures out why you act like you do. The only problem is that the animal psychiatrist is a *two*-legged who can't even speak our language. Did you ever hear of anything so ridiculous?"

"It doesn't make much sense," Geraldine agreed.

"If the psychiatrist were a dog, he would say, 'Why do you run madly around in circles, Bertram?' and I would say, 'Because my large legs and paws and body need more exercise and my head needs more excitement in my life.' And then he would explain to my owners that I need to live on a ranch somewhere. But of course, if he were a dog, my owners would never understand what he was saying, so simply running madly around in circles won't work. I have to have a *reason*."

"And the reason this morning is me," said Geraldine.

115

"Of course. There I am, sound asleep, my body going to pot, and all at once I hear this cat's voice and I'm *off*. Exercise time! Of course I have to bark, too, to make it look authentic. My owners hear all the barking and carrying on. They look out the window and see *you*, and they say, 'Oh, it's just a cat that's got Bertram riled up this morning,' and they go back to eating their toast. So everyone's happy."

"Except the cats," said Geraldine.

"That's true," said Bertram. "Not the cats. In order for me to get any exercise without being hauled off to a psychiatrist, I have to scare cats and kittens half out of their minds. It's a hard job, I tell you, but I have to do it."

Geraldine didn't quite buy that, however. "So why did you *have* to go up in Murphy's loft and tear up the place? What were you trying to prove when you did *that*?"

Bertram flattened his belly against the ground even more, and his tail hugged his bottom all the tighter. "Well, sometimes I'm just plain ornery, I guess. It seemed a good time to show my master how tough I can be, so that when I go berserk in the yard, he'll think it's all because I hate cats."

"But what if we had been in there when you came roaring up the steps? Would you have flung us about the place the way you did those old boots and socks and rags?"

"I don't know," said Bertram. "Sometimes I sort of do what the spirit moves me to do. If you cats didn't jump when I barked, if your tails didn't slash and your fur didn't fly, everyone would laugh at me. I can just imagine the songs the Cat Quartet would sing about me at the Fishmonger if I couldn't frighten anyone."

He got up at last, stretched himself, and yawned.

"And so, you see, we go on doing what we do best. I bark and chase around, you cats tremble and arch your backs, and the world goes 'round. If I didn't bark and run, if you didn't hiss and scratch, why . . . I don't know what would happen. The sun would cease to shine, maybe."

"Whatever," said Geraldine. "But just remember this, Bertram. If you ever bark and leap a little too close to me, you will get a scratch across your nose you wouldn't believe."

"Don't try me," Bertram said, a low growl coming from his throat. "Chasing cats is about the only excitement an old dog like me gets any more."

Geraldine leaned a little closer. "And if the scratch across your nose doesn't work, I'll do something worse. I'll send Old Henna to come and get you."

At that the hair on the back of Bertram's neck bristled, and he began to tremble. "Where have I heard that name before?" he whimpered. "And why does it make me shake?"

"Ah," said Geraldine. "It seems that all creatures, indoors and out, have heard tales of Old Henna in their younger years. All animal mothers, I guess, use the old witch cat to frighten their young into obedience. Just behave yourself, Bertram, or she'll come for you, don't think she won't! But I tell you what. If it will make you feel any better, I'll walk the perimeter of the fence a time or two, and you can bark and run your legs off."

"Much obliged," said Bertram, his fur flattening down again.

117

So Geraldine got up and began walking paw over paw around the top of the fence surrounding Bertram's yard. Bertram, predictably, raced around madly, barking his head off.

The back door of the house opened and the master stepped out on the porch.

"What's he barking at this time?" came the voice of Bertram's mistress from inside.

"Just a cat," the master called. "That cat's just asking for it. She's leading him on a merry chase, you can bet."

When the chase was over, Geraldine jumped back down into the alley, where the other cats joined her. It was obvious that even Texas Jake was impressed.

"How did you do *that?*" asked Boots. "I never saw Bertram settle down and listen to anyone. I never saw him put his tail between his legs!"

"I didn't have twenty-nine kittens without learning a little something about discipline," said Geraldine, and led the cats back down the alley in a grand procession to the Fishmonger.

In the parking lot, Geraldine enjoyed telling the other cats about her adventure with Bertram the Bad. But none of them agreed that Bertram was really an old softie at heart.

"Don't let him fool you, "said the Abyssinian. "If you ever had the misfortune to fall into his yard, he'd have your hind leg for supper."

"And your throat for an appetizer," said the Siamese.

"Do you see this scar on my right front paw?" asked the Persian. "He almost killed me once when he escaped from his master. I'm afraid he's pulled the wool over your eyes, Geraldine. It shows what a good actor he is."

"Perhaps," said Geraldine. "But I think it's safe to say that every living creature, even Bertram the Bad, has a little good in him somewhere."

"His little toenail, perhaps," said Boots.

"A single whisker, maybe," said Elvis.

15
INVASION

After the members of the Club of Mysteries had returned to Murphy's garage, the open window of the loft was suddenly blocked of all sunlight as the crow appeared in the opening, then hopped inside, his wings flapping a time or two before he strutted about the floor on his sticklike legs, his beady eyes fixing first on one cat, then on another.

"Trouble," he cawed.

"So what else is new?" asked Texas Jake. "It is always bad news when you're around, Crow."

"Just looking out for you, that's all," Crow replied. "Think where you'd be if you didn't have me keeping a sharp eye out on the neighborhood. I came to tell you that Steak Knife and his gang are on the move, and I have it on good authority that he plans to invade our alley."

"What do you mean, *our* alley?" asked Geraldine. "It's public property. All they have to do is come on over."

"Ah. They don't just want to *come* over," said the crow. "They want to *take* over. They want your loft, Texas Jake. They want easy access to the Fishmonger."

"You mean they want to trade places? They want *us* to live in the dump?" Carlotta cried.

"No, no, no! Not by a whisker of your chinny-chin-chin," said the crow. "Let's just say that they want to expand. Steak Knife would like to be Lord of the Loft, King of the Alley, Commander in Chief, Cat Supreme, and Ruler of the Dump, too. He wants to move his headquarters here and control everything, from the dump at one end of his empire to the Fishmonger at the other."

The low growl that came from Texas Jake's throat filled the loft. The rush of wind that followed the growl was the sound of his breath escaping through his nostrils. "There can be only one Lord of the Loft, King of the Alley, Commander in Chief, and Cat Supreme, and that's me," he hissed.

"Well," said the crow, "don't blame the messenger. I'm merely telling you the news that's going around. Take it or leave it; it's all the same to me. If there's a big fight and any bodies are lying around, I'll find you. I'll be back. Adieu." And off he went out the window, the sound of his flapping wings growing more distant until finally the noise was gone.

"Oh, Texas! What are we going to do?" Carlotta asked, snuggling against him out of terror.

"They're not only after our loft, they're after our tails!" said Polo, beginning to shake, remembering the large collection of rat tails, cat tails, dog tails, fox tails, mouse tails, bird tails, and coon tails that Steak Knife had strung up on the fence around the dump.

"Well, lads," said Texas Jake, looking at the male cats. "It's up to us. Are we going to let the Over-the-Hill Gang simply come in and take over?"

"No!" said Boots and Elvis and Marco and Polo together.

"Don't *we* get a vote?" asked Geraldine.

"What can *you* do?" sneered Texas Jake.

"We can at least vote!" said Carlotta.

"All right. Are we going to let the Over-the-Hill Gang come in and take over?" Texas Jake asked again.

"No," said Carlotta and Geraldine.

"We will need every bit of strength we can muster," said the big yellow cat. "Let us sleep on it tonight, and in the morning we will meet with the other cats at the Fishmonger and draw up a battle plan."

So all the cats snuggled down in their places. Polo, as usual, tried to sleep near his mother, in hopes that she would at least put a paw over him as he slept. But no one seemed able to fall asleep right away. In fact, most of the cats seemed to be lying with their tails tucked beneath them, just in case a tail hunter came by in the night.

"Tell us a story, Geraldine," begged Carlotta. "I sleep much better if someone tells me a story."

"Once upon a time," the mother cat began in her low, raspy voice, "there was an old, old house with an old, old woman in it. And the old, old woman had an old, old cat named Henna—"

"Not *that* kind of story!" said Carlotta.

"No, no, let her tell it! Now that she's begun, I have to hear the rest," said Boots.

So Geraldine went on: "Now, Henna, though she was very, very old, was a witch cat. By day she slept peacefully on the lap of the old, old woman and looked as though she hardly had the energy to purr. But by night she had the strength of a horse. Her eyes shone silver in the moonlight, her brown hair glowed red at the ends. She had claws that curled over the ends of her toes and a tail as thick as a man's arm. And if you had the misfortune to go into the house of the old, old woman at night and walk up those dark, dark stairs . . . Well!"

Polo scooted close to Marco, Carlotta snuggled tighter next to Texas Jake, and Boots and Elvis wrapped their paws around each other and shook so hard that the army cot rattled.

"One day," Geraldine continued, "a robber came to the home of the old, old woman. He tricked her into letting him in, saying he had come to inspect her fireplace. But once inside the house, he emptied her purse. He opened her cupboards and took all her food. Just as he started upstairs to see what jewelry she might have hidden away in an old, old drawer of her old, old dresser, Old Henna rose up on her hind legs at the top of the stairs, showing her terrible claws. Her eyes flashed silver, and red sparks flew off the ends of her fur. She opened her terrible mouth and shrieked like the howl of wind from a witch cave. The robber was blown backward, the robber was blown sideways, and then, with a horrible scream, the robber was sucked forward, right

123

into the witch cat's mouth, and he was never, ever, seen again."

No one in the loft slept very well that night. Every time there was a squeak of a floorboard or a sudden snore, a rattle of the window or a creak of the rocking chair, everyone jumped.

At the Fishmonger the next day, Elvis repeated the story to the Abyssinian, and the Abyssinian repeated it to the Siamese. The Siamese told the story of Old Henna to the Persian, and soon every cat in the parking lot and beyond had heard the tale. It seemed that all the cats remembered hearing something about the Witch Cat when they were small, and all of them glanced nervously about from time to time.

But Texas Jake knew they had a job to do. After dinner that evening, he stood up on the wall of the parking lot and announced that their neighborhood—indeed, their very lives—were in danger. For at that very moment, he said, Steak Knife and his Over-the-Hill Gang were plotting against them, and who knew what the night would bring?

"I'll go on watch tonight," said Elvis. "If you hear me sing like this"—and he gave a high-pitched trill—"it means that I see them coming. One note if by land, two if by rooftop."

"But once they are here," Texas Jake warned, "it means a fight. We must fight tooth and nail until we have driven them out of the alley, lads. And if we fail, the crow will take the hindmost."

"A song! A song!" called the Persian. "We need a battle song to give us courage!"

The Cat Quartet put their heads together and soon came up with a song:

"Over hill, over dale,
We will hit the alley trail,
If old Steak Knife
Comes cruisin'
Along.
In and out, hear them shout,
As we give his gang the rout,
If old Steak Knife
Comes cruisin'
Along.
For it's hi, hi, hee
At the Fisho-mongeree.
Shout out your orders
Loud and strong!
If his gang comes here,
Grab them by the ear,
If old Steak Knife
Comes cruisin'
Along."

They had scarcely finished when the crow flew down out of the sky and cawed, "Soon, fellows, soon!" for he had seen the tall grass moving down by the dump.

Timothy the mouse darted out from behind a trash can lid and said he had a feeling it would be that very night, for he detected a slight tremor in the earth.

"Back to the loft, lads! Everyone prepare to take your

places if Elvis gives the signal: One if by land, two if by rooftop," said Texas Jake.

The cats all recited vows of solidarity—vows to die, if necessary, for the honor of the alley. Back to the loft they went, but not a single eye closed, and every heart seemed to be beating double time.

16
OLD HENNA

Despite their anxieties, some of the cats fell asleep. Carlotta nestled securely between Texas Jake's two front paws, Boots snuggled against Marco, and Polo edged up against his mother, as close as he could get.

Elvis, true to his word, sat at the window of the loft, looking out over the neighborhood.

But a short time later, Polo saw that the sleek black cat was resting his head on his paws. Polo was afraid he was sleeping. He crawled away from his mother and checked on the black cat. Sure enough, Elvis's eyes were closed, and Polo knew that even if he were to waken him, Elvis might fall asleep again, for Geraldine's story of the night before had cost all of the cats some sleep.

This wouldn't do! Someone had to stand guard over the alley. He himself might not be very smart, and he'd never learned to read, but Polo was faithful, and he felt sure he could keep his eyes open for a few hours, at least. So without waking the slumbering black cat, Polo took Elvis's place at the loft window. He knew that at the first sign of movement in the alley, above or below, Elvis was to give the alarm, and every cat in the neighborhood, whether a member of the Club of Mysteries or not, would take up his battle station.

The moon was in and out of the clouds, and when it shone at all, it was only a sliver of its former self. In fact, the moon seemed to be the only thing moving at all. But still Polo stood guard, and the night moved on.

He kept his eyes on the alley. Then on the rooftops. Then on the alley again. Nothing . . . nothing again . . . still nothing. His eyes began to close. No! He mustn't sleep! He opened them wide. They closed again. And once again they opened.

He thought he saw something, but he wasn't sure. Not in the middle of the alley, but behind the garbage cans. Then . . . there they were—a long line of cats. Their bellies hung low to the ground, their tails stuck straight out behind them, their heads were down, and they made not a sound. Polo felt dread from the tips of his ears to the end of his tail.

"Elvis!" he cried, giving him a nudge. "They're here!"

The sleek black cat sprang to his feet and looked to the alley below. At once he gave the alarm—one shrill cry— and immediately the cats in the loft shook themselves awake and leaped up to take their positions. But Steak Knife and his gang were so near there was no time for the other cats in the neighborhood to come to their defense.

The members of the Club of Mysteries would have to defend the loft themselves.

Texas Jake gave the orders:

"Geraldine, crawl under the fur coat; Carlotta, jump up on the hat rack; Elvis, take the old rubber tire; Boots, behind the trunk! Polo will crawl down in the flowerpot, and Marco and I will stand guard at the top of the stairs and attack the first cats who come up. We may be out-numbered, lads, but we'll fight to the finish."

Polo took his place inside the huge flowerpot, his eyes and ears just peeping out over the rim. He was so close to the stairs that he could hear every little sound from below. First he thought he heard a paw-step. Then he smelled the dump—the odor of burning tires and rotting garbage and old tin cans. Steak Knife was coming and bringing the smell with him!

Polo trembled inside the flowerpot. He felt perhaps he should be out there with Carlotta, keeping her safe. And then he thought of his mother. His MOTHER! Who would protect *her* from Steak Knife and his Over-the-Hill Gang, with their sharp teeth and their ragged claws and their shifty eyes, just looking for trouble?

"Mother?" he whispered in the darkness, but there was no answer.

Polo could hear the raspy voice of Steak Knife down below, the raggedy, scraggly cat with scars on his back and legs, and mange on his hindquarters. "I think this is it, mates," the raspy voice said, "the clubhouse of that conceited big-nose cat with the fancy title—Lord of the Loft, King of the Alley, Commander in Chief, and Cat Supreme, my eye! Texas Jake, that's who he is, and when we get through with him, he won't even be Lord of his Little Toe, King of a Catfish, Commander of Anyone, and he sure won't be Cat Supreme. Cat Stew, maybe. Just follow me up the stairs, mates, and we'll see if this is the club where those highfalutin cats hang out. They tell me they've even got one who can *read*! Can you believe that?"

"We'll show them a thing or two," said one of his partners.

"We'll see who's Cat Supreme!" said another.

"We'll tie their tails in knots but good!" said a third.

Crickety-crack went the stairs as they started up. *Snippity-snap* went the floorboards.

Suddenly the air was split with a horrible, hideous sound—half cry, half scream.

Polo's blood seemed to turn to ice. Peeping over the edge of the flowerpot, he saw Steak Knife pause with his left foot in the air as though he had been frozen on the spot. All the cats behind him stopped too, each bumping into the cat ahead of him.

When Polo looked where they were staring, he saw— right there at the top of the stairs, not three feet away from the flowerpot—a horrible, hideous cat standing on her hind legs, her paws outstretched, her claws extended, her mouth open in a terrible howl, her eyes glistening silver, and the ends of her thick hair giving off red sparks in the dark. Such a thick-furred cat Polo had never seen.

Another half scream/half cry filled the loft, and together the cats in the Club of Mysteries and the members of Steak Knife's gang cried out, "Old Henna!"

"The Witch Cat!" rasped Steak Knife.

And suddenly the loft was filled with wails and shrieks and terrible howls as the Witch Cat moved closer and closer to Steak Knife standing on the next-to-the-top step. The raggedy, scraggly members of the Over-the-Hill Gang whirled about and went tumbling, twisting, leaping, spinning, and clawing back down the stairs, their tails as thick as baseball bats.

As the members of the Club of Mysteries ran after them, terrified half out of their wits, they were met by the Persian, the Abyssinian, and the Siamese, who helped them chase Steak Knife and his cohorts up the alley, across the street, and on toward the open field and the woods beyond.

A few minutes later the alley was as empty as a cat's bowl after breakfast. Texas Jake and his little crew stopped to catch their breath, then crept slowly back toward the loft.

"Did you *see* her?" Boots gasped. "She was up there! Old Henna!"

"I could feel her breath on my forehead!" cried Polo.

"I could smell her fur from the hat rack!" said Carlotta.

"I think she scratched my paw," said Marco.

"She took a few hairs from my tail!" said Elvis as they entered Murphy's garage.

Suddenly the cats all screeched again, for coming down the steps toward them was . . . Geraldine!

"Mother!" cried Polo. "Was that *you*?"

"The one and only," said Geraldine. "My, oh my! We gave *them* a fright, didn't we?"

"Madam, they weren't the *only* ones," said Texas Jake,

and Polo thought he could hear the big cat's heart thumping even then.

"Those shrieks!" said the Siamese. "They traveled all the way down the alley. With a voice like that, you should sing in our quartet."

"With a voice like that, she could *be* a quartet," said the Persian.

"Well, Texas, it seems that most of us grew up hearing stories about Old Henna," Geraldine said, licking her fur to make it lie flat again. "Even old renegades like Steak Knife."

"But how did you get your fur to stand up straight like that, Geraldine?" Carlotta asked. "It was truly giving off sparks! Red and orange and white sparks in the dark. I saw it!"

"Oh, that is an old trick," Geraldine said. "We used to play at that as kittens. We would roll around on our mistress's bearskin rug, rubbing our backs hard against it, and then, in the dark, when we bumped against each other, sparks would fly. I'm not sure how. I simply rolled around on that old fur coat to prepare myself."

"Static electricity," said Marco softly. He couldn't help himself.

"Statue what?" asked Texas Jake.

"Never mind," said Marco, not really understanding it himself.

"Then I say let's all go have breakfast at the Fishmonger, lads, and celebrate our latest skirmish."

So they all set off for the Fishmonger, and the Cat Quartet, of course, composed a song in honor of Old

133

Henna. The four cats climbed up on the wall and, after putting their heads together for a considerable time, began to sing:

"Who's that slinking through the dark?
Winding through the city park?
Paws all wet with evening dew,
It's the Witch Cat, coming through.

"Who's that shrieking in the night?
Giving rats an awful fight?
Chill you to the very bone,
Never go outside alone!

"Who's that clawing at the door?
Howling once, then howling more?
Fur as red as noonday sun,
If you see her, run, lads, run!

"Who's that scratching at the glass?
Waitin' for a cat to pass?
She will grab you, 'cause she's tough,
It's Old Henna, sure enough!"

Nobody would ask Geraldine to tell them another bedtime story *that* night!

But back in the loft, it was soon obvious to all the other cats that the Club of Mysteries wasn't big enough for both Geraldine and Texas Jake. Texas Jake was in a terrible mood. It was bad enough, it seemed, when Geraldine had captured the head of the rat pack in her effort to save Timothy. Bad enough that she had helped both Marco and Polo solve the mysteries he had given them. But now, to have chased away Steak Knife and his gang, making them believe that it was Old Henna who lived in the loft, was just too much for Texas Jake to handle.

The songs in her honor! The adulation and fawning and compliments and respect! What was *he*? Chopped liver? Texas Jake seemed to be wondering as he paced the floor, his tail swishing from side to side. How could he be Lord of the Loft, King of the Alley, Commander in Chief, and Cat Supreme with a brass-throated, sharp-clawed, sassy-tongued she-cat who upstaged him at every turn?

Even when he lay down at last in his rocker, even when he put his head on his paws, a low growl issued from his throat with every breath he took.

135

17
CONFRONTATION

It didn't bother Polo in the least that his mother had proven herself the equal of Texas Jake. He loved it that the Cat Quartet sang songs about her and that she was talked about at the Fishmonger. What bothered Polo was that he still wanted his mother to show that she really loved him. He wanted more than just getting the fire department to rescue him, more than just giving him a salutary lick on the head once he was down from the steeple, more than just allowing him to snuggle against her at night. Polo wasn't even sure *what* it would take to convince him that she loved him. All he knew was that whatever it was, he hadn't gotten it yet.

Texas Jake, of course, had other things on his mind. The very next day he called a meeting. When all the members of the Club of Mysteries were awake and sat grooming themselves in the spring sunshine that shone through the open window of the loft, Texas Jake made his pronouncement:

"Friends, felines, and countrymen, lend me your ears. . . ." he began.

Polo, of course, wondered just how he was supposed to take his ears off and loan them to Texas, or why Texas would want them, for that matter. But the big yellow cat continued: "A club, as you know, must have a leader—an executive in charge, a cat of the highest order."

Polo noticed that Geraldine's tail was beginning to twitch.

"And a cat of the highest order," Texas Jake continued, "should be addressed as such, to show the proper respect. An executive in charge, a cat of the highest order, for example, cannot be shown the proper respect if he is simply addressed as 'Texas Jake' or, even worse, 'Texas.'"

Now Geraldine's tail was swishing back and forth. Marco noticed too.

"Therefore, as your leader, I want each of you to address me thus in the future: Carlotta, my love, you are to call me 'Lord of the Loft,' not 'Texas.' You, Boots, are to call me 'King of the Alley.' Elvis shall refer to me in the future as 'Commander.' Polo must call me 'Commander in Chief.' Marco, oh cat who can reeeeeeead," purred Texas contemptuously, "will henceforth call me 'Cat Supreme.'"

And when Marco's tail began to swish too, Texas added, "*Exalted* Cat Supreme." Then he turned his big yellow eyes on Geraldine. "And *you*, Geraldine, as the newest member of our club, shall now, forthwith, forevermore, refer to me when you speak as 'Lord of the Loft, King of the Alley, Commander in Chief, Exalted Cat Supreme, and Grand Pooh-bah.'"

Geraldine merely hissed. "Grand Pooh-bah, my paw!"

she said. "You may be big and you may be brave, but you still eat, sleep, and use a litter box like everyone else. You are still a cat—an alley cat, at that—and I will not call you anything but Texas Jake. I suggest that the others do likewise."

Texas Jake leaped off the rocking chair and circled the tabbies' mother, a growl coming from deep inside him. Polo began to shiver and shake, for he remembered when Texas Jake and Marco had fought, but he had never seen Texas fight a she-cat before, and certainly not a *mother*!

"Oh, Lord of the Loft!" cried Carlotta. "Please don't fight with Geraldine! It doesn't become you."

"I agree, King of the Alley," said Boots. "Fighting with a she-cat is beneath you."

"Surely there are other ways to settle this, Commander," said Elvis.

It was evident to both Marco and Polo that the other cats were truly fond of Geraldine and wished her no harm. They waited to see what would happen, prepared to jump on the large tomcat if necessary to save their mother.

Geraldine merely flicked her tail. "If you are as grand as you say, oh Grand Boo-paw or whatever, if you are so clever at giving the rest of us mysteries to solve that risk our very lives, perhaps it is time that *you* solve another mystery to show you still have what it takes to be leader. Maybe it's time that *you* let the rest of us think up a mystery for *you*. If you are Lord of the Loft, King of the Alley, Commander in Chief, Exalted Cat Supreme, and Grand Pooh-bah, you will gladly prove what a brave and wonderful cat you are."

Texas Jake stopped dead in his tracks. "I am afraid of nothing," he said.

"Excellent!" said Geraldine. "Then the rest of us will put our heads together and come up with a mystery worthy of so grand a cat as you."

Now all the cats pricked up their ears, for the idea of assigning their Commander in Chief a mystery was something that had never occurred to them before.

"Fire away!" said Texas Jake bravely. "Take all the time you need. I will simply nap here in my chair."

With that, he hopped back up on the old rocker. He put his head on his paws and closed his left eye, then his right—but not quite all the way.

Marco took over then. "If any speaker would like the floor, let's hear it," he said. "What mystery of life would you like to have solved? Carlotta?"

Carlotta lifted one dainty paw. "Here is a mystery I have always wanted to understand," she said. "Why do two-leggeds wear rings on their fingers and in their ears and chains around their necks?"

"That's not a mystery at all," said Boots. "When two-leggeds are small, their parents sometimes put them on a leash, just as they do to us. Right? They get used to having something around them at all times—a ring, a collar, a belt. The waist, the finger . . . it doesn't matter. It makes them feel secure and protected. Mystery solved."

Carlotta looked at Boots with adoring eyes, and Polo saw Texas Jake's tail give a swish or two, but Boots continued: "The mystery I would like solved," he said, "is what good is a worm?"

139

"Easy," said Polo, thinking of the grandchildren who often visited the Neals. "Two-leggeds like to drop them down each other's necks," he said, and everyone agreed that was reason enough for a worm to exist.

"What *I* want to know," said Polo, feeling more confident of himself now, "is why some two-leggeds drag a tree inside at Christmas. But just let me try to sharpen my claws on it and they hit me with a newspaper."

"They don't just bring it inside, they decorate it," said Carlotta. "And don't even *think* of climbing it."

For a long time the cats thought about this mystery, but no one could think of a reason the two-leggeds would bring a tree inside.

Finally Geraldine said, "Perhaps it is because they are tired of winter. They think if they show their respect for something green, the earth will turn green again."

"Hear! Hear!" cried all the other cats, pleased with that answer. They still, however, had not thought up a mystery for Texas Jake to solve.

"Here's one," said Elvis. "When a two-legged child is sick, a parent puts a stick of glass into his mouth and makes him hold it there. What is that stick of glass, and what does it do?"

"I believe it's called a thermometer," said Marco. "It tells how hot the child is getting inside his belly, and whether his furnace has reached the boiling point. If it has, they give him water and that puts out the fire."

"Ah!" said all the other cats, for that was a most reasonable answer.

Marco, however, did not want Texas Jake to get by with

a mystery he could solve just by lying on his back with his feet in the air and thinking about it. He wanted a mystery that would be as hard to solve as the one Texas Jake had given him.

"What makes an airplane fly?" he said. "That's what I want to know. Is it alive? Does it lay eggs?" At last, he thought, he had a mystery that would be *very* difficult for any of the cats to solve. And if Texas Jake did manage to get into a plane, it might take him so far away they would never see him again.

Up on the rocking chair, Texas Jake's tail slashed back and forth, back and forth.

"I veto," said Elvis.

Marco looked annoyed. "Why?"

"Because we don't *know* any planes. We don't even know where they roost. It would just be a mystery we'd sit around and talk about, and Texas Jake—I mean, our Commander in Chief—would not have to do a thing."

Whup, whup, whup went Texas's tail up on the rocker.

Then Geraldine spoke up. "I have always wondered," she began innocently, "what is at the bottom of those big blue boxes that stand on legs at the street corners."

"The big metal boxes that people put envelopes in?" asked Boots.

"That's it," said Geraldine.

"A trash can," said Elvis.

"I don't think so," said Geraldine. "There's writing on the sides."

"It says 'U.S. Mail,'" said Marco.

"That must be it, Marco. How wonderful to have such

a clever son," Geraldine said sweetly. "I have always wondered what happens to the envelopes when they are dropped into the box. Does the box gobble them up? Is there a stomach at the bottom of the box? A tunnel? Do the envelopes go through the legs of the box and into the ground? I'm sure that our Lord of the Loft, King of the Alley, Commander in Chief, Exalted Cat Supreme, the Grand Pooh-bah would willingly check that out for us and bring us the answer."

Texas Jake's tail lashed so fiercely that Polo was afraid it might fly off. Texas opened his eyes and sat straight up in his chair.

"All right," he grumbled. "I'll do it!"

18
INTO THE BOX

Carlotta was the first to suggest that they all go to the Fishmonger for a bite or two of breakfast first. Perhaps the Cat Quartet would compose a song about their Grand Pooh-bah and what he was about to do. But Texas Jake wouldn't hear of it. He had said he would find out what was at the bottom of a mailbox, and a commander in chief always follows through.

So all the cats traipsed down the steps of the loft and out of Murphy's garage, looking for a blue metal box on a corner.

Marco was feeling somewhat guilty, because he *knew* what was at the bottom of a blue metal box. He had seen a red, white, and blue mail truck once or twice as it drove up to a box. He had seen the driver get out and open the box up in front. He had seen him pull out a big basket of envelopes and drop them into a sack, then put back the basket and drive away.

Either none of the other cats had been so observant, or they were simply keeping their mouths shut. They all proceeded to a quiet street that had a mailbox at the very end. It would not do to choose a box on a busy corner, where two-leggeds would shoo them away.

"Now what?" asked Boots as the cats surveyed the box from behind a large bush. While they were debating among themselves, they saw a woman coming down the street with an envelope in her hand.

"Hello, kitty," she said to Polo, whose tail happened to be sticking out from behind the shrub.

The cats watched as her hand reached over the little ledge at the top of the box and grasped a handle. She pulled the handle forward and a small hinged door opened. With her other hand she dropped the envelope inside the box. Then she let go of the handle and the little door slammed shut.

"Good-bye, kitty," she said to Polo's tail, and she went back up the street.

"Well, lads, I have only four paws, not eight, so if one of you will be so kind as to jump up on the ledge and pull open the little door, I will get on top of the mailbox and look in," said Texas Jake.

It was decided that Polo, being the most nimble of the cats, should be the one to jump up on the ledge, wrap his paws around the handle, and pull. But first they had to get Texas Jake on top of the blue metal box, and that was not easy because of his lame leg. Being the oldest of the male cats, he was a little stiff in the joints too.

Fortunately there was a fire hydrant near the box, and

Texas Jake was just able to make the jump from the hydrant to the mailbox. He almost slid forward, however, because the top of the box was curved and slick, and then he almost slipped backward. But he was, after all, the Commander in Chief, and he soon mastered the art of keeping his balance. When Texas Jake felt quite secure on top of the mailbox, Polo leaped up to the ledge.

It seemed to Polo that somehow he was getting the worst of this mystery-solving. All Texas Jake had to do was lean forward and look inside. But Polo was supposed to wrap both front paws around the shiny blue handle and pull it forward. If he were a two-legged, with hands instead of paws, he could do all sorts of wonderful things. But he was only a cat, though even his mother seemed to forget that.

"Go ahead, Polo," Geraldine said from below. "Wrap your paws around the handle and see if you can pull the door open so that our Grand Pooh-bah up there can get a good look. And don't just tell me there's nothing inside the box, Texas Jake. We want to know every detail of what is at the bottom."

"Rest assured, madam, that I will give you a full accounting," said Texas.

Trying hard to keep his balance on the slippery, shiny ledge, which was only a few inches wide, Polo wrapped first one paw around the blue handle, then the other, and pulled. But the door was heavier than he thought, and he had very little room to move. In trying to pull it open, he found himself slipping off the ledge until he was dangling in midair from the handle.

"Hurry, Texas!" he cried. "I can't hold on much longer."

On top of the blue metal box, Texas Jake leaned forward and lowered his head. "I can't see a thing," he said.

"Well, you have to stick your head inside, O Exalted One!" said Geraldine. "You're staring at the back of the door."

"Hurry!" cried Polo, his legs churning helplessly against the front of the box.

Texas Jake put his paws on the back of the open door, trying to keep his hind legs on top of the box, and leaned forward until his head was completely inside.

"I still can't see a thing. The opening is too far back," he said.

At that very moment, Polo could hold on no longer. He dropped to the ground, the small metal door closed on Texas, and there was nothing to be seen of him but two hind legs, a tail, and a yellow rear end sticking out the door of the mailbox.

It was simply too much for the other cats. The sight of their Commander in Chief—the rear end of him, anyway—bobbing in the breeze, his tail swishing, his hind legs kicking, sent them rolling on the ground in merriment, muffled howls and meows escaping from their throats.

"Idiots! Imbeciles!" cried Texas, his voice echoing around inside the box. "This door has trapped me. Polo, get up here and open it again."

"I'll try," Polo choked, struggling to control himself.

"See if you can help him out, Polo," Geraldine said, and howled some more.

There was almost no room on the ledge this time because the door was half open, but somehow Polo managed to get up there. Once again he wrapped his paws

147

around the handle and pulled, but this time he went spinning off the edge of the ledge, unable to hold on for even a second. The hinged door slammed shut, swatting Texas Jake on his big yellow behind and pushing him into the blue metal box. He landed at the bottom with a thud.

"Moron!" he bellowed from inside.

By this time the cats were meowing in such glee that Boots pawed at the ground in an effort to stop himself. But even if their Lord of the Loft heard, he was trapped inside a mailbox, so what could he possibly do?

"I'm sorry," Polo called to Texas, "but I have only four paws, not eight, and I can't do the impossible."

"Quit complaining, Texas," Geraldine called out next. "Now that you're in the mailbox, solve the mystery for us. What is at the bottom?"

"Envelopes, envelopes, and more envelopes!" Texas Jake hissed in anger.

"But does the mailbox have a stomach?" Geraldine asked. "Are the envelopes being digested? Are they going down through the legs of the box and into the ground?"

"I'm in a basket of some kind, that's all," Texas reported. "The only thing that's moving in here is me. There is no tunnel going down into the legs of the box."

"Ah!" said Geraldine. "So what is at the bottom of a mailbox is a simply a basket. The mystery is solved."

"Correct," said Texas. "Now get me out of here."

"Oh, was that in the contract?" asked Geraldine in surprise. "Did we *ask* you to go down inside the box? I'm sorry, Grand Pooh-bah, but I don't believe that was part of the bargain. We will, of course, do what we can."

Which was, unfortunately, nothing. For while Polo could easily jump to the ledge again, which he proceeded to do, and open the door with both paws, dangling from the handle as before, there was no way for Texas Jake to climb up out of the box with its slippery sides. The other cats could hear him slipping and sliding on the pile of envelopes, trying to leap toward the open door, but he only hit the inside of the box with a thud and fell back down to the bottom again.

A car pulled up, and a man got out with a handful of letters.

"What's this? A convention of cats?" he said, laughing. He opened the door of the mailbox and dropped the letters inside. A pitiful meow came from deep within the box, but it was drowned out by the slam of the hinged door. The man got in his car and drove away.

"Keep trying, Polo," hissed Texas Jake. "Pull open the door again so another cat can come down here. If I had another cat to stand on, perhaps I could reach the opening."

"And trap *another* cat down there? I don't *think* so!" said Geraldine.

"Well, are you going to just stand around out there, or what?" Texas growled.

"I'm afraid we've done about all we can do," Marco told him. "A two-legged will come by eventually and open the box from the bottom. You can get out then."

"How do you know?" asked Texas.

"Because I've seen one do it."

"And when will he come by?" asked Texas.

Marco himself, with great effort, jumped up on the fire

hydrant, then the ledge to read the times for mail pickups that were posted there.

"Five o'clock this afternoon," he said.

"And what time is it now, oh cat who can reeeeeeead?" asked Texas.

Marco looked at the big clock on the tower of the courthouse a few blocks away. "Ten o'clock in the morning," he said. "Don't worry, Commander in Chief. You have only seven hours to wait."

19
GRAND POOH-BAH NO MORE

There was one angry cat in the mailbox.

Texas Jake was as upset over the fact that he was missing breakfast as he was at being trapped. At least some of the growls coming from the blue metal box were from his stomach, not his throat.

"I tell you what, Texas," said Geraldine. "We'll all trot off to the Fishmonger and bring you back some breakfast. We can drop it through the door at the top."

"Well, hurry it up, then," said Texas Jake. And off the cats went.

It seemed very strange, going off to eat breakfast without their Commander in Chief. The other cats in the parking lot wanted to know where Texas was, and Marco found he had to struggle to keep from smiling when he told them that their Lord of the Loft was at the bottom of a mailbox.

For some reason they ate with considerable good cheer that morning. Carlotta rubbed noses with all the other cats, Polo had a second helping of everything, the Cat Quartet sang every song they had ever composed, and without the Cat Supreme watching their every move, they all had an unusually good time.

"Another round of 'She's a Grand Old Cat,' boys!" said the Persian with the big, fluffy tail, and the Cat Quartet repeated the ode they had composed for Geraldine.

Crow flew down to join in the celebration and looked disappointed that Geraldine was eating with such relish and vigor. "I don't think you're as old as I thought you were," he said.

"Maybe yes, maybe no," she told him. "You'd better hang around someone else, Crow. This cat has five lives in her yet."

Finally, when they could delay no longer, each of them chose a morsel of food to take back to Texas Jake. Carlotta took some fried perch, Polo chose a bit of flounder, Marco bit off a hunk of swordfish, Boots chose a piece of salmon, Elvis took fillet of sole, and Geraldine chose a couple of shrimp.

With their tasty offerings hanging from their mouths, the members of the Club of Mysteries headed back to the quiet street and the mailbox at the very end.

Texas Jake let out a loud yeowl when he heard them coming. "What took you so long?" he cried from deep inside the box. "I could have starved in the time it took you to get back here with my breakfast. What were you doing—yammering with the other cats? Listening to the

152

Cat Quartet? Going back for second helpings? *What?*"

The cats all dropped their offerings on the grass, but before Polo could leap up to the ledge to open the hinged door again, Geraldine held up one paw. "Wait a minute," she said. "As the newest member of this club, there's a little something I want to say. I know I haven't been around to witness the many brave things Texas Jake has done as leader of this club, and it's true that most groups need someone in charge. But just because Texas Jake is your leader does not mean that he is a better cat than any of you."

"Who's that talking out there?" Texas Jake demanded angrily. "Is that you, Geraldine?"

"Indeed it is, Texas, and for once you're going to listen to me. A leader earns the respect of his troops not by making them call him fancy names but by his kindness to them. So if you want these tasty morsels we have brought you from the Fishmonger—and they are choice tidbits indeed—I think it's time you revoke your order that we call you by those highfalutin names, starting with Your Exalted Grand Pooh-bah."

"What?" cried Texas Jake. "You dare say this to me?"

"I dare indeed," said Geraldine. "Be sensible for once. If cats have to call you by those impossibly long names when they speak to you, they'll soon stop speaking to you at all. And where will *that* leave you, oh Pooh-bah Dooh-bah?"

There was silence from inside the mailbox. Geraldine jumped up on top of the box with the shrimp in her mouth, and while Polo dangled from the handle to keep the little door open, she set the shrimp on the back of the opened door and called down, "Is it agreed, Texas, that we can dispense with Your Exalted Grand Pooh-bah and all that other nonsense?"

"We'll even sing a song in your honor," Elvis promised.

And down inside the mailbox, a hungry yellow cat caught the aroma of boiled shrimp.

"Oh, all right, just drop them down, will you?" Texas Jake growled. "But make that song good!"

Geraldine, however, was better at making up stories than she was at composing songs. "One, two, shrimp for you," she said.

Polo let go of the handle and dropped to the ground. The hinged door snapped shut, flipping the shrimp down inside the box.

Marco jumped on top of the mailbox next, taking Geraldine's place. Again Polo leaped up to the ledge, grasped the handle with his front paws, and dangled off the ledge while Marco placed his offering of swordfish on the door.

"Three, four, shut the door," he said. And Polo dropped to the ground.

Carlotta placed her pieces of perch on the open side of the door next. "Five, six, fried fish sticks," she sang.

And Boots said, "Seven, eight, here's your plate," and dumped his offering inside.

"Nine, ten," began Polo.

"Stop! Stop!" cried Texas Jake from inside the mailbox. "This is supposed to be a song in my honor? Where's my name in all this? It sounds like an ode to my stomach."

Elvis took over. "How about this one?" he asked.

"There once was a leader named Jake,
Who liked his fillet of sole baked.
The fish came by mail
And, wiggling its tail,
It flipped itself back in the lake."

"That's not even an ode to my stomach! That's an ode to a fish!" Texas Jake protested.

At that moment a man walked up to the box with a handful of mail and saw all the cats gathered there. When he opened the hinged door of the box, he said, "Whew! It smells sort of fishy in there." He dropped his letters inside.

"Meow!" came a cry from within.

"What's that?" said the man, looking around. "How did one of you guys get in *there*? Is it possible?"

"*Meow!*" came Texas's voice again, angry and urgent. The man reached into his pocket and pulled out his cell phone. He punched in a number.

"There's a cat trapped in a pickup box at the end of Locust Street," he said into the cell phone. And when he put it back in his pocket, he said, "Well, cats, I know you can't understand me, but they're going to send someone by here and get your buddy out."

And sure enough, it was not long before a red, white, and blue truck pulled up to the curb. The driver got out and looked at all the cats sitting around the mailbox.

"Now, how in the world did one of you get inside *that*?" he said. The man in the blue uniform took a key out of his

155

pocket. He knelt down by the box and put the key in a hole. A door at the front of the box fell open, and out sprang Texas Jake, his fur standing on end, a hiss coming from his throat.

"Hey! Hey! Take it easy! *I* didn't put you in there!" the two-legged said, jumping back and laughing. "How you got in there, buddy, we'll never know, but you're out now, so you cats skedaddle."

The cats were only too happy to do just that. They made their way back to Murphy's loft with Texas Jake in the lead, his tail swishing all the way.

When he was up in his rocker again, he surveyed the little group on the floor below, and his tail continued to slash. He clearly was not at all happy with the way his day was going.

"I suppose you are quite proud of yourself, Geraldine," he said. "But, true to my word, I found out what is at the very bottom of a mailbox. A basket, no more, no less. You may call me anything you like. You may call me Texas or Jake or T. J. or just 'Hey, you!' But make no mistake; whatever name you know me by, I am still Lord of the Loft, King of the Alley, Commander in Chief, and Cat Supreme."

"Whatever you say, Grand Pooh-bah," said Geraldine. She lay with her head on her paws, one eye closed, the other on Texas Jake. Texas lay with one eye closed, the other on Geraldine. And throughout the night, whenever Polo woke to change position, he could hear the *swish, swish* of a tail, either Texas Jake's or Geraldine's, he couldn't tell.

20
A Mother's Love

Polo was sad. All his life he had dreamed of finding his mother. And now that she was here, he dreamed of doing some courageous thing that would make her love him forever, make her tell him how wonderful and special he was. He dreamed of feeling her wet, rough tongue on his head and paws, and oh!—especially under his chin and behind his ears.

"Dear, dear Polo," she would purr. "How clever you are! How brave! How I do love you." And then she would whisper, "This will be our little secret, but of all my twenty-nine kittens, you were my favorite. All these years I have been looking for you, and now we will be together always."

But he had *not* done anything really special, and she had *not* said that to him. She had proved herself to be a very clever cat indeed, and Marco had probably inherited his smarts from her. What was left for Polo to do that would be greater than anything Marco had done? Marco could read, while Polo didn't even know the alphabet. He didn't even know what an alphabet was. He only heard Marco mention it occasionally.

That afternoon when the other cats were napping, Geraldine said to Marco and Polo, "Where do you two go when you're not here at the club? You both are wearing collars, so undoubtedly someone takes you in."

"We live at the Neals' most of the time," Marco told her. "Mr. and Mrs. Neal feed us twice a day, morning and night, and have taken in two kittens as well."

"We have our ceramic bowls and our water dishes," Polo told her. "We sleep in a velveteen basket, and when the weather is cold, the Neals let us jump up on their laps and sleep while they read in the evenings."

"We were supposed to be house cats," Marco went on, "and indeed we would have stayed house cats forever, except that one night Mr. Neal left the side door open while he was bringing in the lawn furniture, and out we went for the very first time. We felt grass under our paws and saw stars overhead."

"There were lightning bugs and crickets and breezes," said Polo. "It was the most wonderful place we had ever been—the great outdoors."

"The Neals came looking for us, of course," said Marco. "And we were scolded and taken back in. But after that we knew we could never be completely happy locked inside. And so, every month when the moon is full, we sit at the picture window and whine. Mrs. Neal unlatches the door, and we have a wonderful week or so at the Club of Mysteries."

"You should come home with us, Mother," Polo begged. "I'm sure the Neals would let you stay. I would give you half my food if necessary."

"Oh, I'm not sure I was meant to live in a house," Geraldine told him. "I was meant to roam this earth from hill to hill and valley to valley and sea to sea. If I had to stay in the same place for long, I would feel as though I were in a box. But I'm glad to know that the two of you are doing well and have a home with two-leggeds who take good care of you. Indeed, you both look well fed—especially you, Marco—and your eyes and coats are shiny."

Polo stared at his mother in dismay. "Mother, does this mean that you're leaving?"

"Oh, I must," Geraldine told him. "I was meant to have adventures, and there are too many places to go yet and things to see."

Polo felt as though he could not bear it. "After all this time, you won't stay?"

"Don't worry. Now I know where to find you," his mother said. "Every month when the moon is full, you and your friends and that big yellow windbag of a cat, Texas Jake, gather here at the Club of Mysteries. I will be looking in on you from time to time. Once I have been to a new place, I never forget it and can find my way there again."

Polo was too sad after that to think of anything else. The cats napped that afternoon and feasted again that night at the Fishmonger, but all Polo's thoughts were on his mother's leaving, and he had little appetite for food.

Once again he and Marco snuggled down next to Geraldine in the old rag box, but he was reluctant to sleep, wondering if this would be the last time he would ever lie next to that soft-warm, dark-dank, furry-purry, milk-smelling something he called Mother.

Some time in the night, he wasn't sure just when, he felt a rough, wet tongue on the top of his head. It carefully licked him behind each ear, and the dream was so delicious that Polo rolled over on his side, purring loudly. Then the rough, wet tongue moved down the side of his face, licking his cheeks, his nose, and then—wonder of wonders—it was licking him under his chin.

Here she was, his mother, loving him, and he had done nothing at all to deserve it.

"Mother?" he said, afraid perhaps it *was* only a dream.

"Yes?" she said.

"What have I done to make you love me?" he asked.

"Why, you don't have to do anything, Polo," she purred back. "I love you just because you're you. Of all my twenty-nine kittens, you are the most ordinary of all, the truest cat, and that, my dear, makes you special."

Polo snuggled against her soft fur. He drank in her milk-smelling scent. He listened to the beat of her heart and the soft rumblings of her belly. And when he woke again in the morning, Geraldine was gone.

Texas Jake, of course, was ecstatic that she had finally left. His chief rival, the sassy-tongued Geraldine, was gone. It was time, he decided, for all of them to go home to their masters or mistresses, for if a cat is gone too long,

a two-legged might very well decide it is gone for good and find another cat to take its place.

So Marco and Polo said good-bye to the other cats, especially the beautiful calico Carlotta. They rubbed noses all around, and then they set off for home.

"I guess she's gone," Marco said.

"Carlotta?"

"No. Mother. I saw her leave in the middle of the night. She gave me a lick or two on the head, and I felt then that she was going," Marco answered.

"Yes," said Polo, "but she'll be back sometime, now that she knows where we are."

They hopped up over the fence in the Neals' backyard and meowed at the back door, where Mrs. Neal let them in.

"Why, Polo, *look* at you!" she exclaimed. "Usually you two come back from your adventures looking like the dog's breakfast, but this time you—especially you, Polo—look as though you have had a very special bath. Your fur is fluffy, your ears are clean. I've never seen you look better."

Polo knew then that it had really happened. All this time he had been trying hard to impress his mother. And she had waited until he settled down to being himself before she let him know just how special he was.

"What adventures did you have this time?" the kittens, Jumper and Spinner, asked, eager to hear of the tabbies' latest escapades as they climbed into their velveteen basket.

Marco immediately launched into an account of all that had happened in the past ten days—Geraldine in the refrigerator, Marco under the hood of a car, Polo high on a church steeple, and Texas Jake in the mailbox. But Polo just put his head on his paws, smiling to himself, with a purr so contented and deep that only a mother could understand.

About the Author

Though Phyllis Reynolds Naylor's cats are gone now, she occasionally finds one of their favorite toys, or a bag of catnip. And, of course, she still has the gold velvet couch on which they sharpened their claws. She is the author of more than one hundred and twenty books, including the Newbery Medal winner, *Shiloh*, and its two sequels, *Shiloh Season* and *Saving Shiloh*. *Polo's Mother* is the last book in the Cat Pack series, following *The Grand Escape*, *The Healing of Texas Jake*, and *Carlotta's Kittens*.

Mrs. Naylor lives with her husband, Rex, in Bethesda, Maryland. They are the parents of two grown sons, Mike and Jeff, and are the grandparents of Sophia, Tressa, and Garrett Riley.